Enid Blyton

STORIES FOR BEDTIME

Look out for all of these enchanting story collections
by *Enid Blyton*

Enid Blyton

STORIES FOR BEDTIME

Illustrations by Mark Beech

HODDER CHILDREN'S BOOKS

This collection first published in Great Britain in 2022
by Hodder & Stoughton

7 9 10 8

Enid Blyton® and Enid Blyton's signature are registered trade marks
of Hodder & Stoughton Limited
Text © 2022 Hodder & Stoughton Limited
Cover and interior illustrations by Mark Beech. Illustrations © 2022
Hodder & Stoughton Limited

A CIP catalogue record for this book is available from the British Library.

ISBN 978 1 444 96520 9

Typeset by Avon DataSet Ltd, Arden Court, Alcester, Warwickshire

Printed and bound in Great Britain by Clays Ltd, Elcograf S.p.A.

The paper and board used in this book are made from
wood from responsible sources.

Hodder Children's Books
An imprint of Hachette Children's Group
Part of Hodder & Stoughton
Carmelite House
50 Victoria Embankment
London EC4Y 0DZ

An Hachette UK Company
www.hachette.co.uk
www.hachettechildrens.co.uk

Contents

Giant Sleepyhead and the Magic Towers

Giant Sleepyhead and the Magic Towers

JOCK WAS playing hide-and-seek with Mary. He was looking for a good place to hide, when suddenly he saw a little tower, standing among the bracken.

What an extraordinary thing! thought Jock. 'Mary! Mary!' he called. 'Come and see what I've found!'

Mary came running up.

'My goodness!' she said. 'What a funny little tower! Do you think it's magic?'

They went close to it and stood looking at it. It certainly was peculiar. It stood there, square and tall, all by itself among the trees. The top of it rose to the treetops.

'Let's go inside!' said Jock.

'No, look!' said Mary, pointing to a large notice hanging on the door.

NONE BUT FAIRY FOLK
MAY ENTER HERE

'We're not fairies, so we mustn't!'

'Never mind! We might get to Fairyland, and you know you're always wanting to go there!' said Jock.

So, feeling just a *little* bit frightened, the children pushed open the door and went in.

'Oh, there's nothing inside except stairs going up and round and round!' cried Mary.

'Come on, up to the top then!' said Jock. And up the spiral staircase they went, round and round till they were out of breath.

'Here's the top of the tower!' called Jock. 'And oh! Mary, come quick! There's a lovely sort of fairy aeroplane here!'

So there was. It had two seats, and to each seat

there was a pair of blue wings. It wasn't at all like a proper aeroplane.

Jock and Mary were tremendously excited. They climbed into the seats, just to see what it felt like.

Whizz! Whin-n! Whizz!

'Jock! Jock! It's flying!' cried Mary, feeling very frightened.

'Hush, Mary! It's all right. I expect it will take us somewhere lovely!' said Jock, feeling really rather afraid himself.

The fairy aeroplane flew along rather like a bird without a head. The seats were its body, and the wings at each side flapped just like a bird's.

Jock peeped over the side. 'We *are* going to Fairyland!' he shouted excitedly. 'I can see fairies down there!'

Bump! The aeroplane came to a stop beside another tower, rather like the one in the wood. Jock and Mary scrambled out. They went down the stairs and found themselves in a little room. A gnome sat there, writing in a book. He looked up and saw them.

'Good afternoon!' he said. 'That will be two pieces of fairy gold, please!'

'I'm very sorry, but I'm afraid we haven't any gold. We're not fairies, you see,' Jock explained, going rather red.

'Not fairies! Well, then how did you manage to fly here by our aeroplane?' asked the gnome in astonishment.

'We – we found it at the top of a tower in a wood,' said Mary.

'You shouldn't have gone in that tower!' said the gnome crossly. 'It's got a notice on to say it's only for fairies. Well, you'll have to pay for the ride somehow. I shall get a dreadful scolding if I'm short in my payments.'

Mary began to cry. 'How *can* we get the gold?' she wept.

Just then, in came a yellow fairy. She looked at Mary.

'Don't cry, little girl!' she said kindly. 'What's the matter?'

Mary told her the trouble they were in. The fairy listened and looked rather solemn.

'Yes, you must certainly pay the money you owe for your ride,' she said. 'I'll tell you what to do! Go and ask old Giant Sleepyhead in that castle over yonder if he can give you some work to do and pay you for it.'

She pointed to a castle on a hill. Jock thanked her, took Mary's hand, and went out of the tower.

'Cheer up, Mary,' he said. 'It's all right. When we get safe home again, think what a *lovely* adventure it will be to tell everybody.'

They went over fields and down lanes until they came to the castle on a hill. They went up to a huge door, and pulled at a great bell-string. A bell jangled through the castle with a tremendous noise! Mary took tight hold of Jock's hand. She wasn't sure if she would like seeing a giant.

Clump! Clump! Clump! Down the hall came great footsteps, and the door swung wide open. There stood Giant Sleepyhead, an immense giant with kind blue eyes like large saucers.

'Please!' shouted Jock. 'Please can you give us any work to do? We owe some money, and we want to pay it back. The yellow fairy told us to come to you!'

'Come in! Come in!' invited the giant, and led the way into a huge kitchen. He sat down and put the children on to the table beside him.

'Well, *I* don't know what work I can give you!' he said. 'You're much too little to make my bed or sweep my kitchen!'

'Oh, *do* think of something!' begged Jock.

'Well, there's one thing I'd like you to do, but I'm sure you can't,' said the giant. 'I've promised to go to tea with my cousin, Giant Wideawake, today. But I feel so frightfully sleepy, that I'm afraid when four o'clock comes I'll be so fast asleep I shan't wake up to go! Then he will be angry. Now, do you think, if I fall asleep, that I can trust you to wake me?'

'Oh, yes!' promised the children.

'Well, I'll have a nap now,' said the giant, getting on to an enormous couch, 'and mind you don't forget!' He lay back, closed his eyes, and began to snore so loudly that all the plates on the dresser rattled!

'He's quite a nice, kind giant!' said Mary. 'Can't we do something for him, Jock?'

'I'll tell you something!' suddenly said a little voice.

Jock turned round and saw a tiny goblin near him.

'Look on the floor! Giant Sleepyhead broke his necklace this morning, and all the beads fell on the floor. He fell asleep looking for them, and I'm sure he'd be awfully glad to have them all picked up and threaded. The thread's over there, look!'

The goblin pointed to where what looked like a thick rope lay on the floor. Scattered here and there were large round coloured balls with holes in them.

'Oh, those are the beads, Mary! My goodness, aren't they large!' said Jock.

'Sorry I can't help you!' said the goblin. 'I've got to go and polish up a few black beetles.'

He ran off, and Jock and Mary began picking up the huge beads. When they couldn't find any more, Mary held one end of the rope, and Jock slipped the beads on one by one, until all the great necklace was threaded again.

'Ding! Ding! Ding! Ding!' chimed a clock.

'Four o'clock! Quick, wake the giant!' cried Mary.

'Wake up! Wake up! WAKE up!' shouted Jock at the top of his voice.

Snore! went the giant.

Jock hammered on the giant's toe.

'WAKE UP!' he yelled. Still the giant snored.

'Oh, Mary, what shall we do?' said Jock. 'I'll never wake him.'

'Climb up on the end of the couch, and pull his hair!' said Mary. '*That'll* wake him!'

But it didn't! He only snored more loudly than ever.

Then both the children shouted together. Then

they climbed on to his chest and stamped and pulled his beard. But nothing, nothing woke that giant!

'It's no good!' said Mary at last. 'And, oh, dear! It's a quarter to five now! He'll be *much* too late for his tea party!'

Just then the giant moved. He stretched himself, yawned, and opened his eyes. He looked at the clock, then jumped off the couch in a great hurry.

'QUARTER TO FIVE!' he roared. 'Where are those children who promised to wake me?'

'Here!' answered Jock. 'But we tried and tried and we *couldn't* wake you!'

The giant hardly listened. 'It's *too* bad!' he cried. 'You needn't think I'll pay you a penny piece! In fact, I think I'll give you both a scolding!'

Jock and Mary turned and ran out of the kitchen as fast as they could. They ran into the garden, and there, in the middle of the path, was the little goblin, polishing a black beetle.

'Is he after you?' he whispered. 'Here, get down

this trapdoor! It's so small, Giant Sleepyhead can't use it! Go down the steps till you come to the Shining Cave!'

He lifted up a little trapdoor, and shut it down quickly after them. They heard the heavy tread of the giant overhead!

Down the stairs they rushed, and then along a twisty, winding passage lit by dim lamps. Suddenly the passage opened out into a great cave.

'The Shining Cave!' exclaimed Jock. 'How beautiful!'

All the walls shone with precious stones and glittered like tiny lamps. There was a small yellow carpet lying in the middle of the cave. Jock and Mary went to look at it.

'Let's sit down and get our breath back!' said Jock.

But no sooner had they sat down than – Swish! The carpet rose into the air, passed through a square hole in the glittering roof, then went up and up through darkness till, bump! It came to rest in the open air on some grass!

'Well! What a surprise!' gasped Jock, scrambling off the carpet.

'Oh, Jock! There's another of those aeroplane towers!' said Mary. 'Let's go and see if we can get an aeroplane to take us home again!'

So off they went. But, oh! Directly they got inside the tower, whom did they see but the cross gnome!

'Well, have you brought me the money?' he asked.

'No,' said Jock. 'I'm afraid not!'

'Then I shall complain to the queen!' said the gnome. He blew a whistle. A crowd of little elves came running in.

'Tie their hands behind their backs and take them to the queen's palace!' he ordered.

Poor Mary began to cry. The elves came forward and tied the children's hands behind their backs.

The cross gnome hustled them out of the door and took them in the direction of a big glittering castle.

As they drew near, they saw a great gate, with a flight of steps leading up to it. The gnome took them up, and the gate opened slowly in front of them.

Inside was a wonderful rose garden.

'Where is Her Majesty?' the gnome demanded of the little gatekeepers.

'In the garden by the lily pond,' they answered.

'Come on,' said the gnome. 'We'll just see what the queen has to say to people who use our aeroplanes and don't pay for the ride!'

'She can't be so horrid as *you*!' said Jock. 'I've always heard she was so kind.'

The gnome led them up a grassy path – and then suddenly Jock and Mary saw the queen.

She was sitting on a cushiony throne by the lily pond, and she looked so beautiful and so kind that Mary wanted to kiss her.

The queen saw them coming.

'Whom do you bring with you, Sativus?' she asked the cross gnome in surprise.

The gnome knelt down.

'If you please,' he said, 'these children have been

guilty of using one of our fairy aeroplanes, and they won't pay for the ride! So I'm short in my payments, all because of two naughty children who meddled with something that didn't belong to them.'

'It isn't that we won't pay for the ride, but we *can't*!' said Jock. 'We did go to Giant Sleepyhead's to try to get some money, but we couldn't wake him up when he told us to.'

'I expect they were too lazy to do as they were told, and wake the giant up,' grumbled the gnome.

'Oh, Sativus, but you know that not even a fairy can wake up Giant Sleepyhead when he is fast asleep,' said the queen. 'You mustn't be unfair.'

'Oh, please, Your Majesty,' said Jock, 'do forgive us and let us go. We won't use things that don't belong to us again.'

'We're awfully sorry,' said Mary.

'Well, I'm sure you wouldn't have used one of our aeroplanes if you'd known you'd have to pay,' said the queen. 'Listen, Sativus. Let these children go, and

I will pay for their ride myself!'

'You darling!' cried Mary, jumping up and down in delight.

So Sativus cut the ribbons from the children's wrists and they were free again.

Suddenly there came a tremendous noise outside.

Clomp! Clomp! Clomp!

'Oh, bother! There's old Giant Sleepyhead! What *does* he want?' said the cross gnome.

'Oh, Jock! Perhaps he's come to give us a scolding!' wept Mary.

Everybody waited to see what Sleepyhead wanted.

'Where's that little boy and girl?' he roared. 'Oh, there they are! Well, I just wanted to say I'm sorry I was so cross. I've just found the necklace they've threaded so nicely, and I've got some money to pay them. The little goblin told me they *tried* to wake me at four o'clock, so everything's all right!'

He gave Mary a piece of gold and Jock a piece of gold, then went off back to his castle.

'Hurray!' cried Jock. 'Now we've got some fairy gold after all! Here you are, Mr Gnome; now we don't owe you anything. Please tell us how to get home.'

'Well, if you'll promise not to use fairy things without permission again, I'll send you home in the aeroplane!' said the gnome.

After saying goodbye to the queen, the gnome took Jock and Mary to the nearest magic tower and they scrambled gladly up the stairs, and jumped into the aeroplane.

'Here we are!' said Jock, as it bumped into the tower in their wood. '*What* an adventure we've had, Mary!'

They raced home and told Mother all about it, but, would you believe it, next morning when they took her to the wood to show her the tower – it was gone!

'Oh, they've moved it, so's we shan't go in again!' said Jock.

And I think that must have been why it was gone, don't you?

The Cold, Cold Nose

The Cold, Cold Nose

ONE VERY cold night Pat the cat crept for warmth into the dogs' kennel, where the two dogs, Bobs and Sandy, lay close to one another. There was straw piled high in their kennel, and it was warm and cosy there. Pat crept close to Bobs and curled up between his front paws.

His nose touched her neck, and it was very wet and cold. 'Oh, Bobs!' she said. 'What a cold nose you have! Why have you?'

'All dogs have when they are well,' said Bobs, yawning. 'Shall I tell you why? Or are you too sleepy? It all happened a long, long time ago.'

'Well, tell us then,' said Sandy, who loves a story as much as you do. And this is the story that Bobs told.

'Once upon a time, when the world was young, there came a great flood on the earth. It rained and it rained, and it didn't stop day or night. Now there were some good and sensible people who knew that there would be a flood, so they had built a big ship for themselves, an Ark to float on the water.

'It was a very big Ark, made of good timber by Noah and his sons; it was so big that it could hold two of every animal on earth – lions, tigers, horses, cats, giraffes, pigs, moles, mice, birds, insects, everything. Noah made two of each walk into the Ark when the floods began, and, of course, there were two dogs as well.

'All the animals settled down together, and Noah and his wife looked after them well. When they looked out of the Ark they could see nothing but water, and still the rain went on raining every day and night.

'Now, of course, the dogs were watchdogs, just as

every dog is now. They knew that it was their job to see that everything was safe and sound each night before they settled down to sleep. So one dog went round one side of the Ark every night and the other dog went round the opposite side, each sniffing into every corner to see that there was nothing wrong.

'And then there came a night when one dog heard a peculiar little gurgling sound in a corner of the Ark. He ran to see what it was – and what do you think? There was a hole in that corner and the water was coming in! It was gurgling in fast, and the dog was afraid that the Ark might be flooded and sink.

'So he stuck his blunt little nose into that hole to fill it up and stop the water from coming in. He hoped the second dog would come to look for him and find what he was doing. But the other dog was fast asleep. So the brave animal had to stand still with his nose to the cold, wet hole all night long! In the morning Noah found him there, cold and tired, his nose still pushed into the leak.

'The hole was soon mended and the Ark was safe – but from that day to this all dogs have had cold, wet noses! Just feel them and see!'

The Tricks of
Rag and Tag

The Tricks of
Rag and Tag

ACORN TOWN was very much excited. A new little toadstool house had grown up under the big oak tree, and two pixies had taken it. They had hung out a sign from their house, and on the sign was written this:

RAG AND TAG,

FASHIONABLE SHOEMAKERS.

WE SERVE THE QUEEN OF FAIRYLAND

Well, that made all the folk of Acorn Town feel pleased. To think that the queen's own shoemakers should come and settle in their little town! And what fun it would be to buy the same sort of shoes as those worn at court! They would feel very proud when they went to visit their friends in the next village, for very few of the pixies there wore any shoes at all.

Everybody watched Rag and Tag's shop while it was being got ready. In the window were put all sorts of lovely little shoes. Outside, a bench was put, on which Rag sat to sew the shoes. Tag seemed rather lazy and lay in bed till late, but Rag didn't seem to mind making the shoes by himself.

Then the shop was opened, and the pixie folk were invited to come and buy. They took their silver pennies out of the place where they had hidden them, and went along to be fitted for shoes. There were green shoes, red shoes, blue shoes – shoes of every colour and size, so that even old Prickles the Hedgehog found four to fit him.

'*I'll* have a green pair to match my spring frock,' said Skippitty.

'And *I'll* have a pair of blue ones to match the

bluebells I sleep in,' said Tippytoes.

Rag served his customers quickly and well. He fitted them all, and sent them away very proud of themselves. They all felt delighted to think that they were wearing shoes just like the pair that Rag said he had made for the fairy queen.

He charged them a silver penny each, and soon the window of his shop began to look very empty. Tag did none of the selling, but stayed indoors and snored.

'Don't you think Tag ought to help you?' asked Skippitty, seeing Rag hard at work late in the day.

'Oh, he has his own work to do,' answered Rag, with a sly grin.

'*Has* he?' asked Skippitty in surprise. 'I never see him doing any. What *is* his work?'

But Rag wouldn't tell her any more, so she had to go away puzzled.

Now two days after Rag had sold everyone a pair of shoes, Tippytoes lost hers. She was terribly upset about it, for she really had liked them very much.

'I put them inside a bluebell flower when I went to sleep last night,' she said to all the folk who had come to see why she was crying. 'And this morning, when I looked for them, they were gone!'

'Have you looked in *all* the nearby flowers?' asked the hedgehog. 'You might have looked in the wrong one, you know.'

'Yes, I've looked everywhere!' answered Tippytoes sadly. 'But they're quite gone. I shall have to buy a new pair. Oh, dear! They were such a pretty blue too. I'm sure that Rag won't be able to let me have a pair just like them again.'

She went to Rag's shop to see, and to her delight and surprise, he had a pair of blue shoes exactly like the ones she had lost. She paid him a silver penny and danced away with them on.

The next person to lose his shoes was Prickles the Hedgehog. He had gone to sleep in his hole under the roots of the oak tree with all his shoes on his feet, because it was too much bother to take them off.

And when he woke up, they had all gone!

'Snouts and tails!' cried Prickles in astonishment. 'Now what has happened to my shoes?'

He looked everywhere for them, but not a sign of them could he find, and he was very sad when he told his friends what had happened.

'Two silver pennies they cost me,' he groaned, 'and I'm quite sure Rag won't have four more shoes just my size.'

He went to tell Rag about his loss, and to his astonishment Rag picked up four shoes like the ones he had lost, and showed them to him.

'Just finished them yesterday,' he said. 'That's lucky for you, isn't it? If you have got two more silver pennies to give me, you can have them.'

Prickles hurried home in delight, found two more pennies he had hidden among the tree roots, and scuttled back to the shoe shop. He tried on the four shoes and they fitted him just as well as his others had done.

'That's very lucky,' he said to Rag. Then he heard a strange noise coming from inside Rag's house. 'What's that?' he asked in surprise.

'Oh, that,' said Rag, 'that's only Tag snoring. He doesn't have very good nights, you know, so he sleeps during the daytime.'

'Poor fellow, poor fellow,' said the kind-hearted hedgehog, and he hurried away in his four fine shoes.

The next day someone else lost their shoes and the day after that two more people. It was all very puzzling. No one knew where the shoes went to at all. Luckily Rag always seemed to have other shoes just like the ones they had lost, and they paid him more silver pennies for them.

Then Tippytoes lost her shoes a second time! She had hidden them very cleverly one night in a bluebell bud that was not yet opened – but in the morning they were gone again!

She cried bitterly and felt sure that this time Rag would not have any blue shoes that would fit her tiny feet. But he had! She was pleased, but she didn't like spending her third silver penny, for it left her with only two more for a rainy day.

Now when Prickles the Hedgehog heard that Tippytoes had lost her shoes for the second time, he began to feel uncomfortable in case he should lose *his* for the second time too. He hadn't two more silver pennies, and he didn't think Rag would sell him a third pair for less.

It must be some thief who is stealing all our shoes, thought Prickles. *Well, I'm going to write my name very small inside my shoes, so that I shall know them again, if I see them anywhere.*

He wrote his name very small inside each one of his shoes, and then put them on his four feet again. Then he lay down to sleep, and was soon snoring hard.

When he woke up, his shoes were gone! There were his four little feet all bare and cold! Prickles was angry and puzzled. Who was it who was taking the shoes from the folk in Acorn Town? He thought of this person and that, but everybody had had their shoes taken now, so he couldn't think of anyone it might be.

He trundled off to the shoe shop and told Rag what had happened.

'Dear, dear, dear!' said Rag. 'That's very annoying for you, Prickles. I'm really very sorry for you. But never mind, it just happens that I've got four shoes like the ones I made for you last time, and if they fit you, you can have them.'

'It's no good, Rag,' said Prickles sorrowfully. 'I've only got *one* silver penny left, and you charge two for my shoes.'

'Well, I'll charge you one penny this time,' said Rag, 'because I'm very sorry for you, Prickles.'

'That's kind of you,' said Prickles, and he ran home to get the penny. He paid for the shoes, and put them on. They fitted him beautifully, and felt as comfortable as if he had worn them for days. As he slipped them on, he heard Tag snoring away inside the house, and thought what a lazy fellow he was, always leaving Rag to do all the work.

He trotted back home, and on the way he met Skippitty and Tippytoes, and two or three more pixies, doing their morning shopping. They stopped and spoke to him, for they were very fond of the good-natured hedgehog. He told them all about how he had lost his shoes for the second time, as he walked along with them. Suddenly he got a stone in his left back shoe, and slipped it off to get it out. He shook out the stone, and was just going to put his shoe on again, when he saw something that made him stop and stare in astonishment.

He saw his name written very small inside his shoe! Prickles couldn't believe his eyes. He showed it to Tippytoes, and she said yes, it really was his name, and in his own handwriting too!

He took off the other three shoes he had on, and there, written very small in each one, was his name.

'Why, they're my own shoes that I lost!' cried

Prickles. 'I've gone and bought my own shoes again!'

'But how did Rag get them?' asked Tippytoes. 'He was working in his shop last night because I saw him. He lives near my bluebells, you know. I'm sure *he* didn't steal them.'

'Well, we'll soon find out who *did*!' said Prickles. 'Tippytoes, you go to Rag's shop, and tell him that you've thought of a fine new hiding place for your shoes. Tell him you're going to hide them tonight under the third violet leaf by your home. Then we'll all hide ourselves nearby and watch to see who comes.'

Tippytoes did as she was told, and then that night all the pixies and Prickles too, hid themselves among the bluebells. Just at midnight, when they were feeling rather sleepy, they heard a sound. Someone was coming! Slowly he came nearer and nearer and nearer, and the waiting pixies held their breath. And then they saw who it was!

It was Tag, who snored every day away inside that little toadstool house! He began to fumble about among the violet leaves and then took out Tippytoe's shoes.

And just at that moment all the pixies jumped out at him! He was so surprised that he fell right over, and sat down on a baby nettle that stung him hard.

'So it's you, is it?' said Prickles, taking him firmly by the collar. 'All right, Tag, you'll be very sorry for this. Fancy daring to come and sell us shoes, and then stealing them and selling them to us again!'

Tag began to tremble, and when Rag heard a loud knocking at the door and heard Tag's sobs outside, he trembled too, for he knew that his naughty trick had been found out.

The two of them were taken to the fairy king, and he was told all they had done.

'That's the very same trick they played on my court!' cried the king angrily. 'The queen sent them away for it. This time they shall be sent right out of Fairyland, and shall never come back again.'

So Rag and Tag were sent away, and had to leave

behind the big bag of silver pennies they got from the pixies of Acorn Town. The pixies took their money, and divided it fairly among themselves, and gave Prickles the Hedgehog two extra pieces for being so clever as to think of writing his name inside his shoes.

Rag and Tag were soon very sorry for their bad deeds, but they were never allowed back in Fairyland. They could do no other work besides making shoes, so they still went on making them. And people do say that the flowers called ladies' slippers, which I expect you've often picked in the fields, are just bunches of Rag and Tag's shoes tied together, blowing in the wind. Look at them closely next time, and see!

The Very Old Teddy Bear

The Very Old
Teddy Bear

BRUINY, THE teddy bear, was very old indeed. He belonged to Billy, and he was older even than Billy, because once upon a time he had belonged to Billy's mother.

Billy's mother had loved him very much, and she had never wanted to give him away. But when she had a little boy of her own, she brought old Bruiny out of the cupboard and gave him to Billy.

'There you are!' she said. 'You can have old Bruiny, darling. He's so soft and cuddlesome. He's had to be sewn up here – and here – and his ears don't match now, but I expect you will love him because he looks so sweet.'

Billy did love him. He was such a very cuddly bear. You know, some toys are much more cuddly than others and you feel as if you must snuggle them up in bed. Well, Bruiny was that kind of toy. He was lovely in bed.

Billy loved him very much. He played with Bruiny a lot when he was little. Then he came to the time when he liked engines and cars, and he played with those all day.

New toys came to the nursery. There was a very neat sailor doll. There was a clockwork dog that could run and wag its tail. There were two soldiers, both as smart as could be.

They laughed at old Bruiny. 'Whatever does Billy keep you for?' they said. 'A dirty, smelly old toy like you! You look awful. Your ears don't match – and did you know you have lost an eye?'

'Yes. I know,' said Bruiny. 'It fell down a crack in the floor. I couldn't get it out.'

'You ought to be put in the dustbin,' said the clockwork dog in disgust. 'I don't like living in the same toy cupboard as you!'

'He won't be kept much longer,' said the sailor doll. 'Billy will throw him away – he's too old even to *give* away now!'

'Don't let's talk to him,' said one of the soldiers. 'Really, he's quite impossible!'

But the bear didn't seem to mind what they said. He smiled a little, and looked at them out of his one brown eye.

'You don't seem to mind the idea of being thrown away!' said the sailor doll, annoyed.

'I shan't be thrown away,' said Bruiny.

'Well, you might be given away, or thrown into the back of the cupboard and never remembered again,' said the clockwork dog.

'I shan't be forgotten, or given away,' said Bruiny. 'I may fall to bits with old age, but I shan't be put into the dustbin, and I dare say I shall still be here when you are all broken and gone.'

'What does he mean?' said the sailor doll to the two soldiers. 'He seems very sure about things. How does he know he won't be thrown away?'

'He sits there and smiles, and he doesn't care a bit when we say these things to him,' said one of the soldiers, puzzled.

'Dirty, ragged, smelly, ugly old thing!' said the clockwork dog. 'I'd be afraid of the dustbin every minute of the day, if I was like him!'

Bruiny wasn't unhappy or worried. He just looked rather amused, as if he knew something that the others didn't know. They were so curious about it that at last they asked him.

'Why are you so sure that nothing horrid will happen to you?' said the sailor doll at last. 'Tell us. You look as if you know something that we don't know.'

'I do,' said Bruiny. 'I know the biggest thing in the world, the only thing that can be trusted, and the most beautiful thing there is. And I know I am safe as long as it lasts.'

'How are you safe? What do you know? What is the biggest thing in the world?' said the other toys in surprise.

'Listen to me and I will tell you,' said the teddy bear, looking at them out of his one brown eye. 'What do you see when you look at me? I know very well! You see a dirty old bear, sewn up here and there because he got torn, with ears that don't match, and with only one eye, and no growl!'

He stopped. The others nodded. That was just what they did see.

'Well, Billy sees all that too, but it doesn't matter to him, because he loves me,' said Bruiny. 'Love is the very biggest thing in the world, you know. I'm safe because Billy loves me. *He* won't put me into the dustbin, *he* won't give me away. I'm Bruiny, the old bear he loves, the old bear his mother loved too, the old bear that has snuggled up to him hundreds and hundreds of times!'

'Oh,' said the sailor doll. 'He must love you a lot, Bruiny.'

'He does,' said Bruiny. 'I'm a lucky bear, because I've been loved a lot. I've loved Billy's mother too, and of course I love Billy. No wonder I'm happy.'

'Yes. No wonder you are happy,' said the clockwork dog. 'I'd like to be loved like that too. You must feel very safe when you are loved. It's a pity there isn't more love in the world, Bruiny. There doesn't seem enough to go around.'

'There is really,' said Bruiny, 'but we don't all do our share, and love one another. I know you hate me, for instance – but I can't help being old and ragged.'

'No, we don't hate you,' said the sailor doll, looking suddenly ashamed. 'We weren't very wise, that's all. We didn't think about this biggest thing in the world. Please be friends, will you?'

'Of course,' said Bruiny, delighted. 'I'll do anything I can for you – I'll tell you stories of the time when

Billy's mother was a little girl, if you like. I know such a lot of stories.'

But before he could tell them one, Billy came in. 'Where's old Bruiny?' he said. 'Oh, there you are. Come along, Bruiny, I want to cuddle you tonight, because I feel lonely. Mother's gone away for a bit, you know. We'll snuggle up in bed together, dear old cuddly bear!'

'How Billy loves Bruiny!' said the sailor doll to the others. 'No wonder he feels safe. It must be nice to be loved like that. Let's be friendly and loving to him now, shall we? Because he really is such a nice old bear.'

I expect you wonder what has happened to old Bruiny. Well, he belongs to Billy's little sister now, and *she* takes him to bed every night, and loves him. So he knows quite a lot about the biggest thing in the world, doesn't he – lucky old bear!

Chipperdee's Scent

Chipperdee's Scent

ONCE UPON a time the queen of Fairyland emptied her big scent bottle, and asked the king for some new scent.

'I don't want any I've ever had before,' she said. 'Get me something strange and lovely, something quite different from anything I've ever had.'

So the king sent out his messengers all over the place – to the topmost clouds and to the lowest caves – begging anyone who knew of a strange and lovely scent to bring it to the queen. For reward he would give a palace set on a sunny hill, and twelve hard-working pixies to keep it beautiful.

Palaces were hard to get in those days, so anyone who had a lovely scent in a bottle or jar journeyed to the queen with it. But she didn't like any of them. She was really very hard to please.

Now there lived in a cave at the foot of a mountain a clever little pixie called Chipperdee. He spent all his days making sweet perfumes, and he made them from the strangest things. And just about this time he finished making the strangest and loveliest perfume he had ever thought of.

He had taken twenty drops of clearest dew and imprisoned in them a beam of sunlight and a little starlight. He had taken the smell of the earth after rain and by his magic he had squeezed that into the bottle too. Then he had climbed up in a rainbow and cut out a big piece of it. He heated this over a candle flame and when it melted he let it drop into this bottle.

Then he asked a two-year-old baby to breathe her sweet breath into the full bottle – and lo and behold, the perfume was made! It smelt glorious – deep, delicious and so sweet that whoever smelt it had to close his eyes for joy.

Now although he lived in a cave, the smell of this new perfume rose through the air and everyone who lived nearby smelt it. An old wizard sniffed it and thought, *Aha! That is the scent that would please the queen mightily! I will go and seek it.*

So off he went and soon arrived at the cave where Chipperdee sat working.

'Let me buy some of that new perfume of yours to take to the queen,' said the wizard.

'No,' said Chipperdee. 'I am going to take it myself. I shall get a palace for it and twelve hard-working pixies.'

'What do you want with a palace?' asked the wizard. 'Why not let me give you a sack of gold for that bottle of scent? The queen may not like it all – and still you have the sack of gold! I will not ask for it back.'

'You know perfectly well that the queen will love this new perfume,' said Chipperdee. 'Go away, wizard.

I don't like you, and you won't get any scent from me! I start tomorrow to journey to the queen.'

The wizard scowled all over his ugly face and went away. But he made up his mind to follow Chipperdee and steal the scent from him if he could. So when he saw the pixie starting off, he made himself invisible and followed him closely all day long.

Chipperdee felt quite sure that he was being followed. He kept looking round but he could see no one at all. But he could hear someone breathing! It was very strange.

It must be that wizard, he thought to himself. *He's made himself invisible. He's going to steal my bottle of scent when I sleep under a hedge tonight. Ho, ho! I'll teach him to steal it!*

When it was dark the pixie found a nice sheltered dell. He felt all around until he found some little flowers with their heads almost hidden under heart-shaped leaves. He took out his bottle in the darkness and emptied a little of the scent into each flower, whispering to them to hold it safely for him.

Then he filled the bottle with dew and set it beside him, curling up to go to sleep beneath a bush. He pretended to snore loudly, and almost at once he heard a rustling noise beside him, and felt a hand searching about his clothes.

The hand found the bottle and then Chipperdee heard quick footsteps going away. He sat up and grinned. Ho, ho! The wizard thought he had got a fine bottle of scent – but all he had was a bottle of plain dew!

The pixie lay down again and slept soundly. In the morning he woke up, and looked round at the little flowers near him. They were small purple flowers, so shy that they hid their heads beneath their leaves. The pixie jumped up and picked a bunch. He smelt them. Ah! His scent was in the flowers now, and it was really wonderful.

Off he went to the court, and there he saw the wizard just presenting the queen with the bottle of plain dew that he had stolen from the pixie. How Chipperdee laughed when the queen threw it to the ground and scolded the wizard for playing what she thought was a silly trick on her!

The pixie stepped forward and told the queen how the wizard had followed him and tried to steal his rare perfume. 'But, Your Majesty,' he said, 'I poured the scent into these little purple flowers, and if you will smell them, you will know whether or not you like the scent I have made.'

The queen smelt the flowers – and when she sniffed up that deep, sweet, delicious scent she closed her eyes in joy.

'Yes!' she cried. 'I will have this scent for mine! Can you make me some, Chipperdee? Oh, you shall certainly have a palace set on a sunny hill and twelve hard-working pixies to keep it for you! This is the loveliest perfume I have ever known.'

Chipperdee danced all the way back to his cave and there he made six bottles of the strange and lovely scent for the queen. The king built him his palace on a sunny hill, and he went to live there with his wife and twelve hard-working pixies to keep everything clean and shining.

But that isn't quite the end of the story – no, there is a little more to tell. *We* can smell Chipperdee's scent in the early springtime, for the little purple flowers he emptied his bottle into still smell of his rare and lovely perfume. Do you know what they are? Guess! Yes – violets! That's why they smell so beautiful – because Chipperdee once upon a time emptied the queen's scent into their little purple hearts!

What's Happened to the Clock?

'What's Happened to the Clock?

PATSY AND William were busy putting out their railway on the playroom floor. It took a long time because there were so many rails to fit together, and some of them were rather difficult.

'After we've put all the rails out, we'll put up the signals, and the station, and the tunnel,' said Patsy. 'Isn't it a beautiful railway set, William?'

It certainly was. It had belonged to their Uncle Ronnie, and he had gone abroad and had given them the set he had had when he was a boy. He had looked after it carefully and everything was as good as new.

At last all the rails were fitted together, the station

was put up, with little porters and passengers standing on the platform, and the tunnel was placed over one part of the line.

'Now for the signals, and then we can put the engine on the lines with the carriages and set it going,' said William.

Patsy looked at the clock to see what time it was. She gave a cry. 'Oh, dear! Just look at the time. It's only five minutes to our bedtime – and we've just come to the very nicest part of all – getting the train going!'

William frowned. 'This bedtime business! We always seem to have to go to bed just when we're in the middle of something exciting. Yesterday we had to go before we finished the pictures we were painting.'

'And the night before that I couldn't finish the story I was reading,' said Patsy. 'Bother the clock. It goes much too fast.'

'What's Mummy doing?' said William suddenly.

'She's turning out the old chests on the landing,'

said Patsy, looking surprised. 'Why?'

'Well, she won't guess how the time is going then,' said William, and he got up from the floor. He went to the clock and turned the hands so that instead of saying a quarter past seven, they said a quarter past six!

'There!' said William. 'It's only a quarter past six. We've got another hour to play!'

'Oh, William!' said Patsy, shocked. 'You can't do a thing like that.'

'Well, I have,' said William. 'Mummy isn't wearing her watch today because the glass is broken and it's at the jeweller's. She'll come and look at this clock and she'll think it's right, so then we'll have a whole hour extra to play in!'

Patsy didn't say any more. She wanted the extra hour. Perhaps their mother would never guess!

Mother called from the landing after a while. 'Surely it is getting near your bedtime, you two. What does the clock say?'

William looked at it. 'Twenty-five to seven,' he called.

'Really? But surely it is later than that?' said Mother. She popped her head in at the door and stared hard at the clock. 'Dear me – how extraordinary. It does say twenty-five to seven. Has it stopped?'

'No, it hasn't,' said William, not looking at his mother. He suddenly felt rather ashamed. Patsy did too. She turned very red in the face and her mother wondered why.

'Well, I suppose I must have mistaken the time,' said Mother, and went to get on with her turning-out. The children didn't say anything to one another. They both wished they hadn't put the clock back like that – they had tricked their mother, and that was a horrible thing to do.

'Do you think we ought to tell Mummy what we've done?' asked Patsy, after a time.

'No,' said William. 'We've done it and we might as well take the extra hour.'

WHAT'S HAPPENED TO THE CLOCK?

So they didn't say a word to their mother. They went to bed at quarter past eight instead of quarter past seven, feeling rather tired – though the clock, of course, only showed quarter past seven!

Next morning the clock appeared to be quite right again. When the children heard the eight o'clock hooter going, far away in the town, the clock said eight o'clock too. How had it got itself right again? They looked at Mother, wondering if she would say anything about it, but she didn't say a word.

They went to school as usual, stayed there to lunch, and came back to tea. They did their homework and then went up to the playroom to go on playing with their railway. It looked very exciting indeed, all set out there.

'I'll have one engine and you have the other,' said William. They were lucky because there were two engines, and it was fun to set them both going and switch them from one line to another just when it seemed as if there was going to be a collision.

They had played for what seemed a very short time, when Mummy put her head round the door.

'Not much more time,' she said. 'Make the best of what time is left before going to bed.'

The children were astonished. Why, surely it couldn't be more than six o'clock! They had hardly played any time at all! They glanced at the clock.

'Why – it says five past seven!' cried Patsy. 'It can't be five past seven. It simply can't.'

'No, it can't,' said William. But certainly the clock said five past seven. 'Shall I alter it again?' he asked.

'No, don't,' said Patsy at once. 'For one thing, Mummy has seen the time – and for another, I don't want to trick her again. I felt dreadful about that. I think we ought to have owned up when she came to kiss us goodnight – and we didn't.'

They argued about the time for a while, then Mother called from the bathroom. 'What's the time by the clock, children? Surely it's bedtime now?'

They looked at the clock. It said a quarter past seven.

WHAT'S HAPPENED TO THE CLOCK?

'Mummy, the clock says a quarter past seven,' called William. 'But it can't be! What's happened to the clock? I'm sure it isn't right.'

'Dear me – a quarter past seven already,' said their mother. 'Well, you must certainly go to bed then. Just tidy up quickly and come along. You can leave your rails out, of course.'

So the children had to leave their railway before they had set the engines going for more than once or twice round the rails. It was very disappointing.

They had their baths, brushed their teeth and hair, and got into bed. Mother said she would bring them some hot chocolate.

While they were sitting up in bed, still feeling gloomy, William heard the church clock beginning to strike. He listened and counted.

'One-two-three-four-five-six-seven – why, it only struck seven times. It's seven o'clock, not eight o'clock.'

'We've come to bed a whole hour early,' said Patsy.

'Mummy!' called William. 'The church clock has just struck seven. It isn't eight o'clock. It's seven. We've missed a whole hour's play.'

'The playroom clock says eight o'clock,' said Mother. 'You went by that yesterday, didn't you? So you must go by it today.'

Mother sounded rather stern. Patsy looked at her and burst into tears. 'Mummy! We put the clock back yesterday so that we could have a whole hour's extra play. We were horrible!'

'Yes, it was rather horrible,' said Mother. 'I really thought it was just a trick and that you'd own up, you know, when I kissed you goodnight. Then I saw that you really did mean to deceive me. And now the clock has paid you back! It's an hour before its time instead of an hour after.'

'Mummy,' said William, 'I believe you've played a trick, haven't you? If you haven't, what's happened to the clock?'

'Of course I've played a trick,' said Mother,

laughing. 'Exactly the same trick that you played on me, but the other way round. Now drink your chocolate and go to sleep.'

'Mummy, I'm very sorry,' said Patsy, rubbing her eyes. 'I felt quite dreadful about it. I'm glad you played a trick too – now we're quits!'

'Yes, we're quits!' said Mother, and she kissed her and William too. 'You gained an hour and lost an hour and perhaps learnt a lesson – so we won't say any more about it.'

They didn't – and you won't be surprised to hear that the playroom clock has behaved in quite an ordinary way ever since!

The Tale of
Lanky-Panky

The Tale of
Lanky-Panky

ONCE UPON a time there was a great upset in the land of Twiddle because someone had stolen the queen's silver tea service!

'Yes, it's all gone!' wept the queen. 'My lovely silver teapot! My lovely silver hot-water jug! My lovely sugar basin and milk jug – and my perfectly beautiful silver tray!'

'Who stole it?' cried everyone. But nobody knew.

'It was kept locked up in the hall cupboard,' said the queen, 'and it was on the very topmost shelf. Nobody could have reached it unless they had a ladder – or were very, very tall!'

Now among those who were listening were the five clever imps. When they heard the queen say that the thief must have had a ladder – or have been very tall – they all pricked up their pointed ears at once.

'Ha! Did you hear that?' said Tuppy. 'The queen said someone tall!'

'What about Mr Spindle-Shanks, the new wizard who has come to live in the big house on the hill?' said Higgle.

'He's tall enough for anything!' said Pop.

'I guess he's the thief!' said Snippy. 'I saw him round here last night when it was dark.'

'Then we'll go to his house and get back the stolen tea service,' said Pip.

'Don't be silly,' said the queen, drying her eyes. 'You know quite well that if you five clever imps go walking up to Mr Spindle-Shanks's door he'll guess you've come for the tea service, and he'll turn you into teaspoons to go with the teapot, or something horrid like that!'

'True,' said Tuppy.

'Something in that!' said Higgle.

'Have to think hard about this,' said Pop.

'Or we'll find ourselves in the soup,' said Snippy.

'Well, I've got an idea!' said Pip.

'*WHAT?*' cried everyone in a hurry.

'Listen!' said Pip. 'I happen to know that the wizard would be glad to have a servant – someone as tall as himself, who can lay his table properly – he has a very high table, you know – and hang up his clothes for him on his very high hooks. Things like that.'

'Well, that doesn't seem to me to help us at all,' said Tuppy. 'We aren't tall – we are very small and round!'

'Ah, wait!' said Pip. 'I haven't got to my idea yet. What about us getting a very long coat that buttons from top to bottom, and standing on top of each other's shoulders, five in a row – buttoning the coat round us, and saying we are one big, tall servant?'

'What a joke!' said Pop, and he laughed.

'Who's going to be the top one, the one with his head out at the top?' asked Tuppy.

'You are,' said Pip. 'You're the cleverest. We others will be holding on hard to each other, five imps altogether, each holding on to each other's legs! I hope we don't wobble!'

'But what's the sense of us going like that?' said Snippy.

'Oh, how foolish you are, Snip!' said Pip. 'Don't you see – as soon as the wizard gets out of the way we'll split up into five goblins again, take the teapot, the hot-water jug, the milk jug, the sugar basin and the tray – one each – and scurry off!'

'Splendid!' said Tuppy. 'Come on, I'm longing to begin!'

The imps borrowed a very long coat from a small giant they knew. Then Pip stood on Pop's shoulders. That was two of them. Then Snippy climbed up to Pip's shoulders and stood there, with Pip holding his legs tightly. Then Higgle, with the help of a chair, stood up on Snippy's shoulders – and last of all Tuppy climbed up on to Higgle's shoulders.

There they were, all five of them, standing on one another's shoulders, almost touching the ceiling! Somehow or other they got the long coat round them, and then buttoned it up. It just reached Pop's ankles, and buttoned nicely round Tuppy's neck at the top.

They got out of the door with difficulty. Pip began to giggle. 'Sh!' said Tuppy, at the top. 'No giggling down below there. You're supposed to be my knees, Pip. Everyone knows that knees don't giggle!'

Snippy began to laugh too then, but Tuppy scolded him hard. 'Snippy! You are supposed to be my tummy. Be quiet! We are no longer five imps, but one long, thin servant, and our name is – is – is . . .'

'Lanky-Panky,' said Snippy suddenly. Everyone laughed.

'Yes, that's quite a good name,' said Tuppy. 'We are Lanky-Panky, and we are going to ask if we can be the Wizard Spindle-Shanks's servant. Now – not a word more!'

'Hope I don't suddenly get the hiccups!' said Pip. 'I do sometimes.'

'Knees don't get the hiccups!' snapped Tuppy. 'Be quiet, I tell you!'

The strange and curious person called Lanky-Panky walked unsteadily up the hill to the big house where the wizard lived. Tuppy could reach the knocker quite nicely, for it was just level with his head. He knocked.

'Who's there?' called a voice.

'Lanky-Panky, who has come to seek work,' called Tuppy.

The wizard opened the door and stared in surprise at the long person in the buttoned-up coat. 'Dear me!' he said. 'So you are Lanky-Panky – well, you are certainly lanky enough! I want a tall servant who can reach up to my pegs and tables. Come in.'

Lanky-Panky stepped in. Tuppy, at the top, looked

round the kitchen. It seemed rather dirty.

'Yes,' said Spindle-Shanks. 'It is dirty. But before you clean it, you can get my tea.'

'Yes, sir,' said Tuppy, feeling excited. Perhaps the wizard would use the stolen tea service! That would be fine.

The wizard sat down and took up a book. 'The kettle's boiling,' he said. 'Get on with my tea.'

The curious-looking Lanky-Panky began to get the tea. There was a china teapot and hot-water jug on the dresser, but look as he might, Tuppy could see no silver one.

'Excuse me, please, sir,' he said politely. 'But I can't find your silver tea things.'

'Use the china service!' snapped the wizard.

'Good gracious, sir! Hasn't a powerful wizard like you got a silver one?' said Tuppy, in a voice of great surprise.

'Yes, I have!' said Spindle-Shanks. 'And I'll show it to you, to make your mouth water! Then I'll hide it away again, where you can't get it if you wanted to.'

He opened a cupboard and there before Tuppy's astonished eyes shone the stolen tea service on its beautiful tray.

'Ha!' said the wizard. 'That makes you stare, doesn't it? Well, my dear Lanky-Panky, I am going to put this beautiful tea service where you can't possibly get it! I am going to put it into this tiny cupboard down here – right at the back – far out of reach – so that a great, tall person like you cannot possibly squeeze himself in to get out such a precious thing.'

'No, sir, no one as tall as I am could possibly get into that tiny cupboard,' said Lanky-Panky in a rather odd voice. 'Only a very tiny person could get in there.'

'And as I never let a tiny person into my house, the tea service will be safe,' said Spindle-Shanks with a laugh. 'Now, is my tea ready?'

It was. The wizard ate and drank noisily. Lanky-Panky ate a little himself. Tuppy managed to pass a cake to each of the imps without the wizard seeing, but it was quite impossible to give them anything to drink!

That night, when the wizard was asleep, Lanky-Panky unbuttoned his coat and broke up into five little imps. Each one stole to the tiny cupboard. Tuppy opened it. He went in quite easily and brought out the teapot. Snippy went in and fetched the hot-water jug. Pip got the milk jug. Pop got the sugar basin, and Higgle carried the big, heavy tray.

They managed to open the kitchen door. Then one by one they stole out – but as they crossed the yard Higgle dropped the tray!

Crash! It made such a noise! It awoke the wizard, who leapt out of bed at once. He saw the open door of the cupboard – he saw the open door of the kitchen – he spied five imps running down the hill in the moonlight.

'Imps!' he cried. 'Imps! How did they get in? Did Lanky-Panky let them in? Lanky-Panky, where are you? Come here at once, Lanky-Panky!'

But Lanky-Panky didn't come.

'Lanky-Panky has disappeared!' he said. 'The imps have killed him! I shall complain to the king!'

The queen was delighted to get back her tea service.

When the wizard came striding to see the king and to complain of Lanky-Panky's disappearance, the five clever imps, who were there, began to laugh and laugh.

'Would you like to see Lanky-Panky again?' they asked the surprised wizard. 'Well, watch!'

Then, one by one they jumped up on each other's shoulders, borrowed a big coat from the king and buttoned it round them.

'Here's old Lanky-Panky,' they cried, and ran at Spindle-Shanks. 'Catch the wizard, someone, for it was he who stole the queen's things, though he doesn't know we knew it and that we took them back to her!'

So Spindle-Shanks was caught and punished. As for Lanky-Panky, he sometimes appears again, just for fun. I wish I could see him, don't you?

The Donkey Who Bumped His Head

The Donkey Who Bumped His Head

ONCE THERE was a donkey who bumped his head against a tree. He bumped it so hard that he saw stars, and this surprised him very much.

'The stars fell around me!' he cried. 'I saw them, I saw them! This is most important news. I must tell it to Grunts the Pig.'

So he trotted to the other end of the field and put his head over the wall into Grunts's sty.

'Ho, Grunts!' he said. 'The stars have fallen from the sky! I saw them myself this morning!'

'This is most important news,' said Grunts in astonishment. 'Why, the sun might fall next! Let us go and tell Gobble the Turkey.'

So they went across the yard to Gobble the Turkey.

'Ho, Gobble!' they said. 'The stars have fallen from the sky! What do you think of that?'

'This is most important news,' said Gobble in surprise. 'Why, we are none of us safe, if things fall upon our heads from the sky. Let us go and tell Daisy the Cow.'

So they went into the buttercup field and found Daisy the Cow.

'Ho, Daisy,' they said. 'The stars have fallen from the sky! What do you think of that?'

'This is important news,' said Daisy, nibbling a thistle in her astonishment. 'Why, it is dangerous to be out if things like this happen! I wish I could go into my shed. Let us go and tell Baa-Baa the Sheep.'

So they all went up the hill to where Baa-Baa the Sheep was lying with her two lambs.

'Ho, Baa-Baa,' they said. 'The stars have fallen from the sky. What do you think of that?'

'This is most important news,' said Baa-Baa in surprise. 'Why, my little lambs might be hit by one of those stars, and think how frightened they would be! Let us go and tell Koo-Roo the Pigeon.'

So they all went into the farmyard where Koo-Roo the Pigeon was picking up corn grains.

'Ho, Koo-Roo,' they said. 'The stars have fallen from the sky. What do you think of that?'

'This is most important news,' said Koo-Roo in surprise. 'Why, I might have eaten one by mistake, and then I should be very ill. Let us go and tell Old Rover the Watchdog.'

So they all went to the other end of the yard where Old Rover the Watchdog was sitting in the sun outside his kennel.

'Ho, Old Rover,' they said. 'The stars have fallen from the sky. What do you think of that?'

Rover opened one eye and looked at all the animals.

'This is strange news,' he said. 'I have seen no stars falling from the sky. When did they fall?'

'They fell this morning,' said the donkey. 'I had just bumped my head against the big chestnut tree in my field, and at that moment I saw them fall. They were red and green and yellow. Oh, it was a marvellous sight, Old Rover!'

'This is a serious thing,' said Old Rover, with a twinkle in his eye. 'It must be put right. What will all the children do without the stars in the sky at night? They will miss them terribly.'

'Do you think it was my fault?' asked the donkey, beginning to tremble. 'I believe the big chestnut tree touches the sky, for it is very tall – and when I bumped my head against the hard trunk, perhaps the top branches were shaken, and brushed the stars from the sky.'

'Perhaps,' said Old Rover. 'What are you going to do about it?'

'I don't know,' said the donkey. 'Can *you* help me, Grunts?'

'No,' said the pig. 'But perhaps Gobble the Turkey can.'

'I can't,' said the turkey. 'But perhaps Daisy the Cow can.'

'I can't,' said the cow. 'But perhaps Baa-Baa the Sheep can.'

'I can't,' said the sheep. 'But perhaps Koo-Roo the Pigeon can.'

'I can't,' said the pigeon. 'But perhaps Old Rover the Watchdog can.'

'Of course I can,' said Old Rover, yawning. 'Go home, everybody. I'll put the stars back in the sky tonight without fail.'

So everyone trotted off home, and when night came they looked anxiously up into the sky. Sure enough all the stars were there, far too many to count.

'Old Rover is clever,' said the donkey, and he took him a mouthful of straw to lie upon.

'Old Rover is wise,' said Grunts the Pig, and he took him a crust of bread to gnaw.

'Old Rover is wonderful,' said Gobble the Turkey, and he took him a bone he had found.

'Old Rover is splendid,' said Daisy the Cow, and took him a bundle of hay.

'Old Rover is fine,' said Baa-Baa the Sheep, and took him some wool to warm him.

'Old Rover is marvellous,' said Koo-Roo the Pigeon, and took him a biscuit she had found.

'Old Rover is cunning!' said Old Rover to himself as he looked at all his presents. 'Now I shall be chief of the farmyard!'

And all the stars twinkled merrily just as if they were enjoying the joke too.

The Cuckoo in the Clock

The Cuckoo in the Clock

IN THE nursery on the wall hung a cuckoo clock. Every hour the little wooden cuckoo sprang out of the little door at the top and called 'Cuckoo!' very loudly indeed. Then it went back into its tiny room inside the clock and stayed there all by itself until the next hour came.

The wooden cuckoo was very lonely. There was nothing to do inside the clock except look at all the wheels going round, and he was tired of that. He was a most intelligent little cuckoo, and when the nursery children talked near the clock he listened to every word, and learnt quite a lot.

He knew when the bluebells were out in the wood, for he had heard Lulu say that she was going bluebelling. He knew that The Beatles were the greatest performers in the world, for he had heard Johnnie say so a hundred times. And he knew that seven times six are forty-two, because once Barbara had to say it twelve times running because she hadn't learnt it properly the day before.

So you see he was quite a wise little cuckoo, considering that he lived in a tiny room inside a clock all day long. He knew many things, and he longed to talk to someone in the big world outside.

But nobody ever came to see him. The children had heard him cuckoo so often that they didn't think anything about him, and except when Jane the housemaid dusted the clock each morning nobody came near him at all.

And then one night a wonderful thing happened. The little fairy Pitapat asked all the toys in the toy cupboard to a party at midnight! What an excitement there was!

The teddy bear, the sailor doll and the baby doll all got themselves as clean and smart as could be. The wooden Dutch doll scrubbed her rosy face clean, and the Japanese doll tied her sash in a pretty bow. The soldiers marched out of their box, and just as midnight came the fairy Pitapat flew in at the window!

The cuckoo had to pop out at that moment to cuckoo twelve times, so he had a fine view of everything. He thought that Pitapat looked the dearest little fairy in the world – and then, dear me, his heart nearly stood still!

For Pitapat looked up at the clock and saw him! She laughed and said, 'Oh, what a lovely little cuckoo! And what a beautiful voice he has! I must ask him to come to my party.'

She flew up to the clock and asked the cuckoo to come to the party. He trembled with delight, and said yes, he would love to come. So down he flew among the toys and soon he was quite at home with them.

The party was in full swing and everyone was having a lovely time, when suddenly the door was slowly pushed open. Pitapat saw it first and she gave a little scream of fright.

'Quick!' she said. 'Someone's coming! Back to your cupboard, all you toys!'

The toys scuttled back to the cupboard as fast as could be, just as Whiskers, the big black cat, put his head round the door. He saw something moving and made a pounce! And, oh my, he caught poor little Pitapat, who was just going to fly away out of the window.

The cuckoo had flown safely up to his little room in the clock, and he peeped out when he heard Pitapat cry out. When he saw that Whiskers had got her, he didn't know *what* to do! He was terrified of cats – but he simply couldn't bear to think that Pitapat was in danger, with no one to help her at all.

So with a very loud 'cuckoo' indeed he flew bravely down to the floor. With his wooden beak he caught hold of Whiskers's tail and pulled and pulled and pulled. Whiskers couldn't think what it was that was tugging so hard at his tail, and he looked round to see.

In a trice the cuckoo flew to Pitapat and picked her up in his claws. He flew to his clock, and, very much out of breath, put the little fairy down just inside his tiny room. Whiskers gave a mew of disgust when he found that the fairy had gone, and jumped out of the window.

The moon sent a ray of light to the cuckoo, and he could see Pitapat quite plainly. She looked very ill, and was as pale as a snowdrop. The cuckoo felt certain that she ought to be in bed. But there was no bed in his little room!

Then he suddenly thought of the tiny bed in the small doll's house in the toy cupboard. He flew down and asked the sailor doll to get it out for him. It was not long before he had the little bed in his beak, and was flying with it back to the clock.

He popped Pitapat into bed, and then fetched her a

cup of milk from the doll's house larder. She said she felt much better, and thanked him. Then she put her golden head down on the pillow and fell fast asleep. How pleased the cuckoo was that he had rescued her! He thought that she really was the loveliest little creature that he had ever seen.

For a whole week she stayed with him, and they talked and laughed together merrily. The cuckoo felt very sad when the week drew near to an end, for he really didn't know *what* he would do without his tiny friend. He knew that he would be lonelier than ever.

Then a wonderful idea came to him. If only Pitapat would marry him, they could live together always and he wouldn't be lonely any more! But would a fairy like to live in a tiny room inside a clock – with a funny old wooden cuckoo? The cuckoo shook his head, and felt certain that she wouldn't. And a big tear came into one of his eyes and rolled down his beak.

Pitapat saw it, and ran to him. She put her arms

round his neck and begged him to tell her why he was sad.

'I am sad and unhappy because soon you will go away, and I shall be all alone again,' said the cuckoo. 'I love you very much, Pitapat, and I wish I wasn't an ugly, old wooden cuckoo with a stupid cuckooing voice, living in a tiny room inside a clock. Perhaps if I were a beautiful robin or a singing thrush you would marry me and we would live happily ever after.'

'You aren't ugly and old!' cried the fairy. 'And your voice is the loveliest I have ever heard! You are nicer than any robin or thrush, for you are the kindest bird I have ever met! And I will marry you tomorrow, and live with you in your clock!'

Well, the cuckoo could hardly believe in his good fortune! They asked all the toys to a wedding party, and Pitapat bought the cuckoo a blue bow to wear round his neck so that he looked very grand indeed. And after the party they went back to the clock and danced a happy jig together round the little room.

'I can make this room lovely!' said the fairy happily. 'I will have blue curtains at the windows, and a tiny pot of geraniums underneath. I will get some little red chairs and a tiny table to match. Oh, we will have a lovely little house here, Cuckoo!'

She set to work, and she made the dearest little place you ever saw. The cuckoo loved it, and one day when Pitapat had brought a new blue carpet and put it down, he was so pleased that he quite forgot to spring out of his door at ten o'clock and cuckoo!

There was no one in the nursery but Barbara, and she was most surprised to find that the cuckoo didn't come out and cuckoo. She got a chair and put it under the clock. Then she stood on it and opened the little door.

And, to her very great surprise and delight, she saw Pitapat's little room, so colourful and pretty, and the cuckoo and Pitapat sitting down to a cup of cocoa and a biscuit each! Weren't they surprised to see their door open and Barbara's two big eyes looking in!

'Don't tell our secret, Barbara dear!' cried Pitapat. 'We are so happy. *Don't* tell our secret! Please! Please!'

'I'll keep your secret,' promised Barbara. 'But please do let me peep into your dear little house each day. It is so little and lovely.'

'You can do that and welcome,' said the cuckoo, and he got up and bowed.

So every day when there is no one in the nursery Barbara peeps into the cuckoo's home in the clock; and you will be glad to know that she has kept her word – she hasn't told a single soul the secret!

The Lucky Green Pea

The Lucky Green Pea

WHEN LITTLEFEET was going down Twisty Lane, he saw a sack lying right in the very middle of the road. It was a large sack, and when Littlefeet looked into it, he saw that it was full to the top with peas in their pods.

'My!' said Littlefeet. 'Look at that! Someone's dropped it off his cart! I wonder whose it is.'

He lifted it on his shoulder and found that it was very heavy, for he was not very big.

'I'd better go and ask at Mr Straws the farmer's, in case it belongs to him,' said Littlefeet, for he was an honest little fellow.

So off he staggered with the sack of peas on his shoulder. As he went, one of the peapods burst, and a little green pea shot out of the top of the sack, and dropped right down Littlefeet's neck. It tickled him a bit, but he didn't take any notice of it.

He didn't know that it was a lucky pea. It was the only pea in the whole sack that was a lucky one. It was lucky because a witch had passed by the row of peas in the night, and her broomstick had brushed against the peapod. A little mouse had eaten all the peas in it but one, and that was the pea that had dropped down Littlefeet's neck.

He soon came to Farmer Straws's yellow cottage, and shouted for him.

'Hey!' he called. 'Where's the farmer? I've got a sack of peas for him. He must have dropped it on the road.'

'It isn't mine,' said Mr Straws, looking over the wall of the pigsty. 'But thanks for coming all the same. Look, Littlefeet, I've got twenty-one dear little pigs. Would you like one?'

'Ooh, yes!' said Littlefeet, delighted. 'I'd love it.'

So Straws gave him a pink pig with a curly tail, and he went off leading it on a piece of string. He carried the sack too, so he was well loaded.

These peas must belong to Mr Cabbage, the greengrocer, thought Littlefeet, staggering along under the sack. *I'll go and ask him. He'll be most upset if he thinks he's lost them.*

Soon he arrived at the greengrocer's, and Mr Cabbage came out to see him. He was feeding his hens in the backyard, and he was most surprised to see Littlefeet with a pig and a sack.

'Have you come to sell me some peas?' he asked.

'No,' said Littlefeet, putting the sack down nearly on top of the pig. 'I found them and thought they were yours, so I brought them along.'

'That was kind of you,' said Mr Cabbage. 'But they're not mine. I haven't any at all. I sold a sackful to Dame Jolly this morning, and maybe they are hers. She took them away in her little cart, and I expect they've dropped off.'

'Oh, dear!' sighed Littlefeet. 'I'd better go there then.'

'Wait a minute,' said Mr Cabbage kindly. 'Have a drink of lemonade and a cake. And look, Littlefeet, do you see all my nice young hens? I've too many, so if you'd like one for yourself, you may take one.'

'Ooh, *thank* you!' said Littlefeet, full of joy. He sat down and had some homemade lemonade and a piece of ginger cake. Then, taking the sack on his shoulder again, he went off with the pig and the hen running beside him.

After some time he came to Foxglove Cottage, where Dame Jolly lived. He knocked at her door and she opened it.

'I've brought the peas you lost,' said Littlefeet, rather out of breath.

'I haven't lost any!' said Dame Jolly in surprise. 'I sold my sackful to Haha Wizard who lives on Sailing Hill.'

'Bother!' said poor Littlefeet, putting the sack

down, and just missing the hen. 'I felt certain it must be yours. I've tried Farmer Straws, and Mr Cabbage, and now you!'

'I'm so sorry!' said kind Dame Jolly. 'Come in for a moment. I'm making some strawberry jam, and I'd like you to taste it.'

'Ooh!' said Littlefeet, who liked strawberry jam better than any other kind. He went indoors, wiped his feet, and waited till Dame Jolly had put some jam into a saucer for him. He ate it with a spoon. It was simply delicious.

'Nicest jam I've ever tasted in my life!' he said.

Dame Jolly beamed with delight.

'You must take three jars with you,' she said. 'I'll make a parcel of them and tie them on the piglet's back, because you certainly won't be able to carry them.'

'Thank you very much,' said Littlefeet. So Dame Jolly wrapped three jars up tightly in some newspaper, and then tied them firmly on to the piglet's back. He squealed and jumped about, but soon he was used to the load and trotted beside Littlefeet quite happily. The hen went too, and Littlefeet called goodbye to Dame Jolly.

In an hour's time he arrived at Haha Wizard's, and thumped at the door. The wizard came to the door and peeped out.

'Here are your peas,' said Littlefeet. 'You must have dropped them in the road.'

'So I did, so I did,' said the wizard. 'Well, I wanted them to put into a spell, but I've done without them now. I don't like peas for eating, so I wonder if you'd mind keeping them yourself?'

'Ooh!' said Littlefeet, who simply loved peas for dinner. 'Yes, I'd love to have them, and thank you very much!'

'Not at all, not at all!' said Haha Wizard. 'You're doing me a kindness, I assure you. Good day!'

He shut the door and Littlefeet staggered off again, full of delight. This time he went home. The piglet carried the jam in a very jaunty manner and the hen ran along beside him.

When he got home it was teatime. He had spent the whole day carrying the heavy sack about! He had had no dinner, and he felt very hungry.

I'll cook myself a whole lot of peas! he thought. *They will make a lovely meal. Just fancy, I've got enough peas to last me a whole week and more. Oh, what a lucky pixie I am! And I've got three jars of new strawberry jam, a little pig and a nice little hen. This has been a lucky day.*

He soon had a fine tea ready. There were green peas cooking, a new loaf, the strawberry jam and a pot of tea. And then, would you believe it, the little hen laid him a nice brown egg!

'Just what I want!' cried Littlefeet joyfully, and he boiled it for his tea.

When he undressed that night the little lucky pea fell out and rolled down a crack in the floor.

'What was that?' wondered Littlefeet. 'It can't have been a button, because they're all on. Oh, I'm sure it wasn't anything that mattered!'

He didn't even look for it, which was a pity – but still, he had had enough luck to last him for a whole year, and there wasn't a happier little pixie in all the village that night than Littlefeet. He fell asleep, and dreamt of green peas and strawberry jam, little hens and little pigs – and when he woke up and remembered that his dreams were true, he chuckled very loudly indeed!

Hotels for the Birds

Hotels for the Birds

'IT'S COLD!' said Harry, shivering. 'Mother, I do hope you've put another blanket on my bed. I was cold all last night.'

'Yes. I've put another one on,' said Mother. 'It really is colder than ever today. All the puddles are frozen, and so is the pond.'

'I don't like this wind that creeps in everywhere,' said Katy, shivering like Harry. 'I'm glad our dog has a good kennel, Mother, with plenty of warm straw.'

'Can't he come indoors to sleep these cold nights?' asked Harry.

'Oh, no – he's as warm as toast in his straw,' said

Mother. 'I got him some fresh straw the other day because his had got rather flattened. You must remember that animals have thick fur coats.'

'And birds have feathers,' said Katy. 'Mother, don't the birds feel cold at night? Where do they roost?'

'In the bushes mostly,' said Mother. 'But the wind must creep through those, and freeze the poor little things.'

'I shall put out my doll's house,' said Katy. 'I shall leave the front door a bit open and then all the birds can go in there to roost.'

'Silly!' said Harry. 'They'd never do that, would they, Mother? They are scared of strange things.'

'No, I'm afraid they wouldn't creep into your doll's house, Katy,' said Mother. 'But it was a kindly thought of yours. Perhaps you would like to do what I used to do as a child, when it was bitter weather like this.'

'Oh, yes! Tell us what you did!' said Harry.

'Well, I used to go and get the flowerpots out of our garden shed,' said Mother. 'And I used to stuff them with hay or straw – not too tightly, but loosely.'

'What for?' asked Katy, surprised.

'I'm just going to tell you,' said Mother. 'After I had stuffed each one, I went round our garden, and I put a pot here, and a pot there – sometimes under a bush, sometimes in a tree, sometimes in a ditch.'

'Oh! For the birds to sleep in, do you mean?' asked Harry. 'Mother, what a lovely idea! I shall do it this very day!'

Mother laughed. 'I hoped you would,' she said. 'Well, you know where the flowerpots are – get the medium-sized ones. You can get straw from Scamp's kennel, or you can get some hay to stuff them with – whichever you like.'

'Hotels for our birds!' said Katy, and that made Harry laugh. They ran off to find the pots. Soon they had about a dozen, and they put hay in six of them and straw in the other half-dozen.

'Now, where shall we put them?' said Katy, as they carried them out of the shed. 'One in the ditch over there – and one in that lilac bush.'

'Yes. And we must remember to be sure not to let the open part of the pot face towards this bitter wind!' said Harry. 'It wouldn't be much good putting down a nicely lined pot in a place where the wind blew into it all night long!'

'No. That's sensible of you,' said Katy.

They had a lovely time putting the pots in good places. In the ditch, in bushes, halfway up the thick ivy on the wall, and in odd corners here and there.

'We've found places for them all, Mother!' said Katy, going indoors. 'Can we go out tonight and see if any birds are sleeping in them?'

'It will take a day or two for the birds to discover them,' said Mother. 'But we certainly will take a torch tonight and go and see – just for fun!'

So that night they put on hats and coats, because the wind was colder still, and took torches to look into the pots.

'Anyone staying in *this* hotel?' said Katy, flashing

her torch into the pot in the bush.

No. It was quite empty. So they went to the next one. 'You must be as quiet as you can,' said Mother. 'We don't want to scare any bird away.'

It was very disappointing, because they found not a single bird in any of their flowerpots – until they came to the very last one of all!

This was in the ditch. Katy shone her torch into the pot – and there, his head tucked well into his wing, was a small robin redbreast! He took out his head, blinked at the light, and then put his head back again under his wing.

'Oh, how lovely!' whispered Katy. 'It's the robin we feed on the bird table every day, I'm sure it is! Oh, I'm *so* glad we found *one* of our pots with a visitor inside!'

That was a week ago. Now the birds have found their new 'hotels' and each night half the pots have visitors.

A blackbird sleeps in the one in the bush. A thrush sleeps in another. Two little blue tits cuddle together in the pot hidden in the ivy – how you would love to see them!

The robin sleeps always in the same pot, down in the ditch, and a little wren is in one nearby. Yesterday there was a hedge sparrow in another pot – I wonder what visitors there will be tonight!

Isn't it a lovely idea? I expect you will put 'hotels' for the birds in *your* garden on wintry nights, won't you?

The Magic Needle

The Magic Needle

TRICKS AND Slippy were tailors. They made coats and cloaks for all the little folk in Breezy Village and the other villages round about.

'We don't get paid nearly enough for our work,' grumbled Tricks. 'We ought to get ever so much more!'

'Yes. If we were paid properly, we should have a nice little motorcar by now to deliver all our goods,' said Slippy.

'Oh, you and your motorcar. You're always talking about that,' said Tricks. 'Now, what I want is a lovely little boat to sail on the river.'

'Fiddlesticks!' began Slippy, and then he had to

stop because a customer had just come in. It was Jinky the gnome. He flung a coat down on the table.

'Look there!' he said. 'Bad work again! All the buttons fell off in a day, and this collar has come unstitched. No wonder we don't pay you top prices, you're so careless!'

He stalked out, looking very cross.

'Blow!' said Slippy, picking up the coat. 'Now I've got to sew those horrid little buttons on all over again. I wish we had a magic needle, Tricks. That's what we want. But nowadays nobody ever hears of a thing like that.'

'A magic needle!' said Tricks, looking up in excitement. 'Why, my old granny used to have one. She did, she did! I'd forgotten about it all these years, but now I've suddenly remembered it.'

'Goodness! A real magic needle?' said Slippy, amazed. 'Where is it?'

'Well, I suppose my old granny has still got it somewhere,' said Tricks.

'Go and ask her to lend it to us,' said Slippy at once.

'Ooooh, no, I wouldn't dare. She doesn't like me,' said Tricks. 'She says I'm always up to tricks, and she shouts at me whenever she sees me, so I never go to see her now.'

'What a pity,' said Slippy. 'Shall I go and see her? She might show me the needle, mightn't she – and oh, Tricks! I've just thought of a most wonderful idea!'

'What?' said Tricks. 'I don't really think much of your ideas, you know.'

'Listen, I'll go and visit your granny and I'll get her to show me the needle – then I'll take her needle and put one of our needles in its place! See?'

'Yes! Yes, that's quite a good idea,' said Tricks, pleased. 'I know the size it was – and it had a very big eye, I remember. I believe I've got one that looks just like it!'

He hunted about in his box of needles and took one out. 'Here it is – just like Granny's magic one – except that there's no magic in this one!'

'Does the real magic one sew all by itself?' asked Slippy.

'Oh, yes – it sews and sews and sews. You've only got to place it on top of a pile of cloth, and say "Coats" or "Cloaks", or whatever you want, and the needle sets to work at once, and hey presto, there's a pile of coats sitting there before you know where you are!'

'Does it cut the cloth up too, before it sews it?' asked Slippy, astonished.

'Not exactly,' said Tricks. 'It sews the cloth into the right shapes – sleeves and so on – and then all the bits and pieces fall away, the coat turns itself inside out, and there you are!'

'Marvellous! Wonderful!' said Slippy. 'I'd simply love to see that happening.'

'Well, you will if you go to see my granny,' Tricks said with a grin. 'But be very careful of her when you go, because she's very fond of scolding people.'

Slippy set off the very next day with Tricks's needle in a needle case. He caught the bus and went to

Hush-Hush Village. He soon came to the house of Tricks's grandmother, a lovely, neat little place with pretty curtains in all the windows.

The old lady didn't seem very pleased to see him. 'Hm!' she said. 'So you're a friend of my grandson, are you, Slippy? Slippy by name and Slippy by nature, I wouldn't be at all surprised. What have you come for?'

'Just to see you,' said Slippy. 'Tricks has said such a lot about you. He said you were such a nice old lady, and so very friendly and kind.'

'Hm! Did he tell you I've been kind enough to scold him a hundred times for his bad ways and mischievous tricks?' said the old lady. 'Tell him to come and see me again, because I've got scolding number one-hundred-and-one waiting for him.'

Slippy began to think that Tricks's grandmother wasn't a very kind old lady.

'Er – is it true that you once had a magic needle?' he asked, thinking that he had better find out before some kind of scolding came his way.

'Quite true,' said the old woman. 'Look in the bottom drawer of that chest, in the left-hand corner, and you'll see a pincushion. The needle is stuck in it. Bring it out and I'll show you what it can do.'

Slippy found the needle easily. He took it out of the pincushion excitedly and gave it to the old woman. She threaded it with red cotton, pulled Slippy's lovely new red hanky out of his pocket and stuck the needle into the corner of it.

'Doll's dress,' she said in a loud voice. And, to Slippy's enormous surprise, that needle set to – and, in no time at all, there was a beautiful little doll's dress lying on the table, all neatly trimmed and finished! The needle had slipped in and out so fast, with a long red thread behind it, that Slippy had found it quite difficult to follow.

'Marvellous!' said Slippy. 'But what about my lovely new hanky? You shouldn't have made a doll's dress out of it.'

'Don't you talk to me like that,' said the old lady, as

if she was going to shout at Slippy. 'You'll just have to blow your nose on a doll's dress, that's all. And if you dare to . . .'

Slippy fled! He pushed the red doll's dress into his pocket. He was grinning broadly. Aha! He had just had time to exchange the two needles! He had the magic one in his needle case – and he had left the one he had brought, safely pushed into the pincushion!

Tricks was delighted when Slippy showed him the needle. 'Well done, Slippy!' he said. 'I never thought you'd be able to get it. Granny's eyes are so sharp, I was sure she'd spot you exchanging the needles. Now we'll be able to make some money. Goodness, we'll really be able to make some money! My word, we'll be able to make a dozen coats a day now!'

'I didn't like your granny,' said Slippy. 'She was rather rude to me. I thought she was going to start shouting at me.'

'She probably was,' said Tricks. 'Well, we will never, never go near her again, so we won't have any more trouble from her. Now – let's go out and buy all kinds of cloth, and get that needle to start working on new coats tonight.'

So out they went and spent a lot of money on new cloth. They staggered home with it and set it on the table.

'Yellow cloth, red cloth, blue, purple, black, green and orange,' said Tricks. 'My, what a wonderful lot of handsome coats we'll have! Needle, listen to me. Here are reels of cotton to match each cloth. You are a sensible needle, and will take the right cotton from each reel. I will thread you the first time, and after that you will thread yourself, just as you used to do for my granny!'

'Most remarkable,' said Slippy, watching him in delight. Tricks threaded the magic needle with red cotton and then stuck it into a pile of red cloth.

'Coats!' he said, and dear me, you should have seen that needle! It flew in and out, in and out, and there were the two sleeves and soon the collar was made, and the lapels, and the coat itself – then the sleeves were sewn in, quick as lightning.

'Buttons! We've forgotten to buy the buttons,' said Slippy suddenly, and he rushed out to buy buttons of all colours. The needle was wonderful with buttons. It sewed them all on in the right places, as quick as a flash and as strongly as could be!

'There's the first coat,' said Tricks, pleased. 'And look at all the bits and pieces that have fallen off just as if they'd been cut away. Really, this is a very powerful needle.'

'It is,' said Slippy. 'Shall we have our supper and go to bed? I don't really want to watch the needle making coats all night long. It's rather tiring to see something working so hard.'

So they had buns and cocoa and went off to bed, leaving the magic needle flying in and out as if it was worked by lightning!

What a marvellous thing!

They fell asleep in their two little beds. The needle

went on working by itself in the workroom. In three hours it had finished the pile of coats – sixteen beautifully finished coats lay in a heap, with shiny little buttons down the fronts.

The needle had no more cloth. It took a look round with its one eye. Ah, what about the tablecloth? It must make a coat out of that. So it did – and a very nice little check coat it was!

Then it took another look round. Ah, what about that hearth rug? That would make a fine warm coat!

And down swooped the needle and in about ten minutes there was no rug to be seen – but in its place was a very warm little coat, with snippings on the floor around it!

The needle was really enjoying itself tremendously. It made coats out of the curtains. It tried to make one out of a cushion, but it couldn't. It made coats out of the dusters, and tea cloths, and even out of a pair of stockings. Really, it was a remarkably ingenious needle.

Soon there was nothing left downstairs for it to sew. So it flew upstairs, looking round with its one eye. When it saw all the bedclothes on the two beds it was simply delighted!

And very soon it was busy making coats out of all the sheets and blankets on Slippy's bed. But as Slippy was lying fast asleep in them, it made things very difficult for the needle. It had to join all the coats together around Slippy, and in the end the bed looked like an enormous sack with sleeves sticking out of it here, there and everywhere! Slippy couldn't be seen – he was inside somewhere!

He woke up and began to wriggle. Whatever had happened? Where was he? He called out to Tricks. But Tricks was now being sewn up too, in half a dozen coats which were made up of his sheets and blankets, and even one of the corners of his eiderdown. Oh, dear, oh, dear!

Slippy and Tricks shouted and wriggled and they both rolled off their beds with a bump. What a dreadful night they had! The needle couldn't quite understand what had happened and kept going up to them and pricking them. That made them yell all the more!

They rolled to the door. They bumped all the way down the little flight of stairs – *bumpity – bumpity-bump-bump*!

But they couldn't undo themselves, because when that needle sewed, it sewed very well indeed!

'Slippy! We'll have to roll out of the door and into the front garden,' gasped Tricks at last. 'We simply must get help. It's morning now, because I can hear the milkman coming.'

He rolled himself hard against the door and it burst open. Out went Slippy and Tricks, looking most peculiar all sewn up in sheets and blankets, with long sleeves flapping about all over the place!

The milkman was amazed. He dropped his milk can and stood there, staring.

'Help! Help!' he shouted. 'There's something very strange going on here!'

Well, very soon the neighbours came out and found out just what had happened. Tricks told them about the antics of the magic needle, and begged his friends to snip the stitches and let him out.

At last he was freed from the mass of sheet-and-blanket coats, and stood up, blinking in the sunlight. And, oh, dear – when he saw his curtains and rug and tablecloth and everything else made into coats, he wept loudly. So did Slippy.

'The needle's still busy!' cried Slippy suddenly. 'Look, it's got into our chest of drawers and it's making coats out of our vests and pants and trousers and everything!'

'We'll have to take it back to my granny,' said Tricks, tears streaming down his face. 'Come on. It's no good, that needle will go on and on till it's taken back. We'll be ruined!'

So they had to take the needle back. How they hoped the old lady would be out. But she wasn't! She was watching for them. She knew that Slippy had exchanged the needles – her eyes were just as sharp as the eye of that needle!

Well, you can guess what happened, and why Slippy and Tricks went home howling and looked sorry for themselves for a whole week. Nobody would buy the coats the needle had made – they said they were afraid of magic coats. So it didn't do them much good to play a silly trick like that on Tricks's grandmother – in fact, they are still trying to undo the stitches in the curtain-coats, and rug-coat and tablecloth-coat, to get them back again.

That needle has taught them not to be lazy, anyhow!

The Forgotten Rabbit

The Forgotten Rabbit

DUMPY WAS a little blue rabbit with a pink ribbon round his neck. He belonged to Belinda, and she was very fond of him. All the toys were fond of him too, for he was a kind and cheerful rabbit, always ready to squeak for anybody when he was pressed in the middle.

One day Belinda took him out to tea with her. She went with her mummy to visit Mrs White and her two little boys, Allen and Peter. They were rough boys, and always wanted to play games of burglars or bandits which Belinda didn't like at all. She would much rather play at tea parties or shopping, so she didn't very much enjoy going to tea with Allen and Peter.

As soon as the two boys saw the little blue rabbit, they grabbed him from Belinda's hand and tossed him up in the air.

'We'll play robbers!' they cried. 'And we'll tie the rabbit up to the tree because he has found our cave of riches.'

'No, don't do that,' begged Belinda. 'He is such a little rabbit, he would hate that.'

'Pooh, he's only a toy!' said Allen. '*He* won't mind!'

'Then I shan't play with you,' said Belinda at once. 'I shall take my rabbit and go and play by myself at the end of the garden.'

But Allen and Peter ran away with the little blue rabbit and did just what they said. They tied him up to a tree and pretended that he was their prisoner. He didn't really mind much because he was quite sure that Belinda would fetch him before long and take him home.

But, you know, that was just what Belinda didn't do! She found that Mrs White had a lovely present for her, a workbox full of needles, cottons and bright coloured wools, and she was so pleased with it that she played with it all the time and quite forgot about the little blue rabbit.

Even when it was time to go home she didn't remember him! No, she took her new workbasket under her arm, said goodbye and thank you to Mrs White and went home with her mother without once remembering that she had left the blue rabbit behind!

But when she was going to bed she remembered him. She always took him to bed with her, and dear me, when she thought of him left behind with the two rough boys, how upset she was!

'Mummy, let me get dressed again and go and fetch my blue rabbit!' she begged.

'Of course not,' said her mother, astonished. 'What are you thinking of? Your rabbit will be quite all right with Allen and Peter.'

So poor Belinda had to get into bed without her rabbit, and she was very miserable. All the toys were miserable too, for they were most alarmed to think that the blue rabbit had been forgotten.

'Allen and Peter said they were going to tie him up to a tree for a prisoner,' wept Belinda. 'Oh, I do hope they have remembered to untie him and take him indoors. It might rain and he would catch such a cold.'

The toys put their heads together and whispered to one another as soon as Belinda was asleep.

'What can we do to rescue the little blue rabbit?' said the sailor doll. 'He will die of fright if he is tied up to a tree all night!'

Nobody knew what to do – until at last a deep voice spoke. It was the kite that lived at the back of the toy cupboard.

'It's a nice windy night,' said the kite. 'If you could manage to put me out of the window, toys, I might be able to fly to Allen and Peter's house and look around for the rabbit. Then, if he could hold on to me I could bring him back.'

'But who will untie his knots if he is tied to a tree,' asked the curly-haired doll.

'I'll go too,' squeaked the clockwork mouse. 'I'm small and I don't weigh very heavily. I can easily nibble through the string if our blue rabbit is tied up to a tree.'

So it was decided that the kite and the clockwork mouse should go together. It was a great adventure for both of them. The big white teddy bear dragged the kite to the window and pushed it out, with the little mouse clinging to the bottom of it, with all his might. The wind took the kite at once and off it sailed into the air, its tail of paper strips hanging down below it.

Soon it had flown all the way to the house where the two little boys lived. Then down it swooped into the garden and lay quite still.

'Go and see if you can find the blue rabbit anywhere,'

said the kite to the clockwork mouse in its deep voice.

So off went the mouse, calling 'Blue rabbit, blue rabbit!' as it went.

It ran into a prickly hedgehog and scratched its nose. It fell over a worm, and was frightened by a very large beetle. But all the time it called, 'Blue rabbit, blue rabbit, where are you?'

At last a sad little voice answered in the distance. 'Here I am! I'm tied to a tree!'

The mouse ran towards the voice, and then, by the light of the moon, saw the poor blue rabbit tied fast to a small tree by pieces of string.

'Oh, clockwork mouse, I'm so pleased to see you!' cried the blue rabbit as the mouse ran up. 'I've been tied up here ever since Allen and Peter left me this evening. I've been so frightened. I've seen a big thing with wings that said "Hoo, hoo, hoo!" to me. And a large spider began to spin a web across my nose, and . . .'

'Well, never mind about your troubles any more,'

said the clockwork mouse kindly. 'I'm just going to nibble through this string, so excuse me if I don't talk to you for a minute or two. It's so difficult to nibble and talk at the same time.'

He began to nibble, and very soon the string was in half and the blue rabbit was free.

'How are we going to go home?' he asked.

'By the way I came,' said the clockwork mouse. 'Just wind me up once more, will you, Rabbit, because I'm a bit run down. Then I'll take you to where I left the kite and we'll fly home with him.'

The blue rabbit wound him up and off they went together. They soon found the kite and stood him upright in the wind so that the breeze might take him into the air again. They held on tightly to his tail and very soon they were all three flying in the sky, back to the nursery window where the rest of the toys were waiting for them.

How they all cheered the kite and the brave clockwork mouse when they saw them! How they hugged the blue rabbit and how he hugged them!

'Sh! Sh!' said the sailor doll. 'We shall wake Belinda if we make such a noise. Blue Rabbit, you had better go and climb into the bed beside her, because she cried herself to sleep tonight without you.'

So the blue rabbit went creeping inside Belinda's bed, and snuggled down there to go to sleep. And there Belinda found him in the morning!

She couldn't believe her eyes!

'Mummy!' she cried, sitting up in bed and holding up her rabbit. 'Mummy! Here's my little blue rabbit back again! Did you fetch him for me last night when I was asleep?'

'No, I didn't,' said Mummy, quite puzzled. 'You must have brought him back yourself, Belinda, without knowing. He couldn't have come home by himself.'

Belinda looked across at the toy cupboard where all her toys sat, waiting to be played with. The sailor doll winked an eye slowly at her, and Belinda understood.

'The toys rescued him, Mummy!' she cried. 'They

did! Sailor doll winked at me just now so he knows all about it!'

'Nonsense!' said her mother. But it wasn't nonsense, was it?

Pippitty's Pink Paint

Pippitty's Pink Paint

ONCE UPON a time the queen of Dreamland thought she would like to have a lovely new nursery for her little baby girl.

'You see,' she said to the king, 'the old nursery doesn't really get enough sun, and babies do need such a lot of sunshine. Couldn't we have a beautiful new nursery built on the south side of the palace?'

'Anything you like, my dear,' answered the king. 'So long as you're happy, that's all that matters. Do you want me to order the nursery now?'

'Yes, please,' said the queen, 'and I want all the decorations to be a perfectly sweet pink, to match the new curtains I've bought for the cradle and the windows.'

'Pink!' said the king. 'Can't you choose some other colour? You know what a trouble we had to match the pink you chose for the drawing room last year. I really don't want all that bother again!'

'It must be pink,' answered the queen.

'All right,' said the king, 'only I hope to goodness the pink curtains you've bought won't be hard to match. I'll call the Lord High Chancellor and give him orders to do what you want.'

'You're a perfect darling,' said the queen, and kissed the king on the tip of his nose.

Well, in a week's time there was nothing but hammering and chattering going on by the south side of the palace. The workmen were tremendously busy, and because they loved the queen, they worked quickly and well, so that before many weeks had gone by, the new nursery was built, with big glass windows in, and a lovely fireplace. 'Please, Your Highness, what colour does Her Majesty the Queen want the decorations to be?' asked the head workman one day, when the Lord High Chancellor came by. 'We're ready to paint the walls now.'

'Her Majesty wants the walls to match the curtains she has chosen,' said the chancellor. 'Wait a minute while I look in my pocket. I've got a pattern somewhere to show you.'

He gave the workman a piece of pink silk. 'That's the colour,' he said. 'Can you get that shade of pink?'

The workman looked at it. 'I don't know if we've got any paint that colour,' he said. 'It's a lovely pink, but not a usual shade. I'll see if I can mix some.'

He went away and tried all day to get a shade of pink to match the pattern of silk – but he couldn't. His workmen tried too, but no one could get a perfect match.

At last the head workman took his paint to the queen and asked her if it would do.

'Goodness me, no!' cried the queen. 'It's a very bad

match; I couldn't possibly have that! The paint *must* match the curtains exactly.'

'My dear, couldn't you buy some other curtains to match the paint?' asked the king. 'That seems to be a much better idea. It would save a lot of trouble.'

But the queen wouldn't hear of it. At last one of her ladies-in-waiting stepped forward and curtseyed.

'If you please, Your Majesty,' she said, 'there is a clever little elf called Pippitty, who lives in Cuckoo Wood. He is an artist and paints the most lovely pictures. I think if you asked him, he could mix you the colour you want. He has the most lovely colours in the world, and he always makes them himself.'

'That's a splendid idea!' said the queen. 'I'll send him a pattern of pink silk at once, and ask him to bring me the paint as soon as he can!'

So a messenger was sent off to Cuckoo Wood, carrying a piece of pink silk with him. The Pippitty Elf was sitting outside his oak tree house painting a picture of the bluebells that grew all around it, and he was most excited when he heard what the messenger had to say.

'I haven't any paint that will exactly match,' he said, 'but I can easily mix some by tomorrow, and I'll bring it to the palace when it's ready.'

He scurried off to pick pink wild rose petals. Then he begged a red ruby stone from the goblins who live in the caves under Breezy Hill. He bought a pink sunset cloud from the Sunset Fairies, and then he hurried home.

He melted the ruby in a big saucepan over a magic fire, pounded up the pink rose petals, and emptied them into the saucepan too. Then he stirred in the little pink cloud, and boiled them all up together. He went and asked Witch Wimple to say a pink spell over the saucepan, and the paint was made!

'It's just exactly the colour of the silk pattern,' said Pippitty proudly, as he set the paint on the window sill to cool.

Next morning he started off, carrying his paint with

him, and soon arrived at the palace. He was shown into the throne room where the king and queen were both sitting.

'Oh, have you brought the paint I ordered, Pippitty Elf?' asked the queen. 'Bring it here and let me see it.'

Pippitty climbed the steps up to the throne and showed his precious paint to the queen.

'Oh, how lovely!' she cried. 'It's just exactly the colour. I *am* so glad. What would you like in return for it, Pippitty?'

'Please, Your Majesty, one thing,' answered Pippitty eagerly. 'Will you let me paint the new nursery myself? I can paint beautifully, and I'll do my very best for you, truly I will.'

'Very well, Pippitty, you shall!' said the queen, smiling. Then she turned to the chancellor.

'Take the Pippitty Elf to the head workman,' she commanded him, 'and tell him Pippitty is to paint the walls himself.'

So Pippitty was marched off, swinging his pot of

paint, feeling as proud as a peacock.

He began to work at once, and everyone came to watch him. He was a clever little elf, quick and neat, and had a funny way of singing while he worked. He had a lovely, bird-like voice, and everyone liked to hear him.

> '*Up and down*
> *And to and fro,*
> *This is the way*
> *The paint should go!*'

he sang, and soon all the people watching joined in his song and sang it with him.

'It *is* a lovely pink you've got!' said the palace servants. 'How did you make it?'

Pippitty told them.

'Clever Pippitty Elf!' they cried. 'How we wish we could make paint like you, and come and paint the queen's new nursery!'

Now Pippitty soon became conceited. He boasted of the paints he had made, he boasted of how cleverly he could paint, and he boasted of how wonderfully he had decorated the nursery. The queen was sorry to see how vain he had become, but because he really had made the nursery look perfectly sweet, she didn't scold him.

'Pippitty, you had better stay on at the palace a little longer,' she said when she came into the nursery on the day that Pippitty finished it. 'There may be one or two other things I should like painted pink too.'

So Pippitty stayed on, very pleased indeed. He had his meals in the kitchen with the palace servants, and because he was a merry little fellow, they spoilt him more than ever.

Pippitty longed to do something else to make everyone think him more wonderful still. He thought and thought what he could do, and at last he had a splendid idea.

'I'll paint all the potatoes pink!' he decided. 'I'll go

down in the cellar with my paint tonight, and take them out of the baskets one by one and paint them. They're so dirty. The head cook will be ever so pleased to find them all pretty and pink. He will think me very clever.'

So that night the naughty little Pippitty Elf crept down to the cellar with his paint and a lit candle. He sat down on the floor, took out the potatoes one by one, and began painting them.

'They *do* look lovely!' he said, as he carefully put them back. 'Oh, I'll paint some with pink stripes and some with dots. That will make a change!'

So he painted pink stripes on some potatoes, and pink dots on others, and very strange they looked. Then he crept up the stairs again, blew out the candle and went to bed.

Next morning the head cook and a kitchen maid went down to fetch up the day's potatoes. They came up the cellar steps, carrying the basket between them. Directly they got into the kitchen the head cook happened to look down at the potatoes.

'Oh, OH, *oh!*' he cried. 'Mercy on us! What's happened to the potatoes?' and he let go his side of the basket in a great hurry.

Clitter-clatter-clutter! All the pink potatoes rolled over the kitchen floor.

'They've gone bad! They've gone bad!' shrieked the kitchen maid, dropping her side of the basket too.

All the servants came running in.

'Whatever in the world is the matter?' they cried.

'Oh, OH! Just look at those awful potatoes! Somebody's worked a spell over them, certain sure.'

Just then in came Pippitty, and stopped at the sight of the floor covered in pink potatoes. He looked round at all the servants and saw that instead of being pleased, they were frightened. He went rather red and picked up a potato.

'Don't touch it, Pippitty Elf!' cried the head cook. 'We don't know what's happened to these potatoes.'

'Well, *I* do!' said Pippitty. 'I painted them all with

my beautiful pink paint. Surely you can see it is my lovely paint that makes these potatoes look so pretty.'

'*Pretty!*' snorted the head cook. 'Do use your sense, Pippitty. Pink paint is all right on walls, and all wrong on potatoes. You've been very silly. Pick up all these potatoes and peel off their foolish pink skins.'

Poor Pippitty felt like crying. He picked up all the potatoes and peeled them. At the end of the morning, he felt more cheerful.

Never mind! he thought to himself. *Everybody makes mistakes. I'll think of a better idea soon.*

But the next idea he thought of was really very naughty. He went into the palace yard to throw the potato skins to the hens. When he saw them rushing about to pick up the peel, he noticed four white hens among them.

'Those white hens lay the eggs that are given to the queen's baby girl,' said a gardener to Pippitty.

Oh, are they now? thought Pippitty. *Now, suppose I painted those four white hens pink – would they lay pink eggs? And how pleased the queen would be to see her baby girl eating pink eggs in a pink nursery off a pink plate!*

Pippitty fetched his paint and a nice new paint brush. He waited until all the servants and gardeners were at dinner, and then he caught each of those white hens and painted them pink from their beaks to their tails!

'There! You look lovely!' said Pippitty, as he finished the last hen and let it go. He went to put away his paint just as the gardeners came back from their dinner.

One of them carried a pail of corn for the hens. He was just going to open the gate of the henhouse, when he stopped still and stared and stared as if he could hardly believe his eyes.

'What's the matter, Meryll?' asked another gardener.

'Oh, oh! Dear me! There's something wrong with my eyes!' said Meryll. 'There's four pink hens in there!'

'*Pink hens!*' said the second gardener scornfully. 'Where?'

Then *he* saw them, and he stared as if he had suddenly seen the moon fall out of the sky!

'I don't like it!' cried Meryll, and he dropped the pail of corn, and turned and ran away! But just round the corner came the Lord High Chancellor.

Bump! Straight into him ran the gardener and knocked him down flat.

'Bless me!' panted the chancellor angrily when he got back his breath. 'What do you mean by this, Meryll?'

'Your Highness. Your Highness! Come and look at something strange!' begged the frightened gardener, helping the chancellor to his feet and dragging him off to the henhouse.

'Pink hens!' gasped the chancellor. 'What in the world made them go pink? What an amazing thing!'

Just then Pippitty came trotting by to have another look at his pink hens. He was very pleased to see the chancellor there.

'Good afternoon, Your Highness,' he said. 'How do you like my pink hens? I painted them this morning so that they will lay pink eggs for the queen's baby girl.'

'Pink eggs and pink potatoes,' roared the chancellor angrily. 'So you're the elf who paints potatoes and hens pink, are you? The head cook complained about you this morning. Come here!'

And poor Pippitty was punished by the chancellor.

'I didn't do it to be naughty,' he grumbled. 'I only did it because it was a good idea. I HATE that old chancellor. I *will* be naughty now, and I'll do something bad to him, yes I will.'

Pippitty went to bed that night feeling very cross and very miserable. In the middle of the night he jumped out of bed, took his pot of paint and crept out of the room.

'I'LL PAINT THAT OLD CHANCELLOR'S BEARD PINK!' said Pippitty. 'That'll teach him to punish me when I'm not naughty.'

He listened outside the chancellor's door, and heard him snoring hard. He crept into the bedroom and made his way to the bedside. Then quickly and neatly he painted the chancellor's long grey beard, until by the light of the moon it gleamed as pink as a spray of almond blossom!

It looked so funny that Pippitty began to laugh, and he had to slip out of the room very quickly, in case he woke the chancellor. He went back to bed, feeling much better, and wondered what would happen in the morning.

When the chancellor awoke and looked at himself in the glass, he couldn't believe his eyes. A pink beard! Whoever heard of such a thing? How dreadful he looked! He couldn't possibly go down to breakfast!

But the poor chancellor always had to be in the breakfast room to see that the king and queen had everything they wanted, and to take any orders from the king before breakfast. He tried washing his beard, but not one scrap of pink could he get off.

At last he finished dressing and went downstairs,

hoping he would not meet anyone. But he met two footmen and the butler, and they all stopped and stared at him in amazement.

'Excuse me, Your Highness,' said the butler, 'but are you feeling quite well?'

'*Perfectly* well, thank you,' answered the chancellor crossly, and went on down the stairs.

He got to the breakfast room just before the king and queen came in. He took up his place behind the king's chair, and waited, trying to pretend he couldn't hear the giggles of the servants in the room.

In came the king and queen. The queen saw the chancellor first and caught hold of the king's arm.

'My dear!' she whispered. 'What's the matter with the chancellor this morning?'

The king looked at him. Then he smiled broadly. 'Ha, ha, ha!' he laughed. 'So you've dyed your beard pink to match the nursery, have you, Sir Chancellor! I'm sure it's very kind of you.'

'Your Majesty! I wouldn't *dream* of doing such

a thing!' said the chancellor, going as red as a
penny stamp. 'A trick has been played on me while
I was asleep!'

The king tried to look stern.

'But who would dare to dye your beard pink?'
he asked.

'It isn't dyed, it's painted!' said the chancellor.
'It's that wicked Pippitty Elf, Your Majesty, the one
who painted the nursery walls pink. He painted all the
potatoes pink, and four white hens too, yesterday.
And because I punished him, he's painted my beard
pink too!'

The king felt very cross to hear of Pippitty's
pranks, but he couldn't help thinking the chancellor
looked very funny and he had to smile whenever he
saw his bright pink beard.

'Fetch the Pippitty Elf here!' he commanded. 'He
certainly can't be allowed to stay in the palace a day
longer. He'll be painting my hair pink next.'

Pippitty was brought in, looking rather scared, and

wondering what was going to be said to him.

'How *dare* you paint my Lord High Chancellor's beard pink?' said the king to the trembling little elf.

'Please, oh, please, Your Majesty, he punished me when I wasn't naughty,' wept Pippitty. 'I only painted the hens pink to make them lay pink eggs for the darling baby princess. I didn't mean to be naughty.'

'Well, you must leave the palace at once,' said the king. 'I was going to let the chancellor punish you again, but if you really didn't mean to be naughty the first time, you can count that one as a punishment for this last naughty trick of yours.'

But the queen was sorry for Pippitty.

'Go and use your paint to make something beautiful, and then bring it to me. Perhaps we will forgive you then,' she said.

So Pippitty went out into the fields very sad and sorry, except when he remembered the chancellor's pink beard, and then he smiled a little smile. He carried his pink paint all day, without finding anything he could make beautiful with it.

At last evening came, and Pippitty sat down in a field and watched the daisies closing up into little white balls.

'They look much nicer when they're open,' said Pippitty. 'They aren't nearly as pretty when they're shut. Oh! I've got a lovely idea! I'll make them pretty while they're shut!'

And he took his paint brush and painted all the tips of the daisy petals pink!

'The pink tip won't show when the daisies open again,' said Pippitty, as he painted away, 'because they will be underneath the petals then, but oh! They do look sweet now!'

When he had finished all the daisies – and it took him many nights – the Pippitty Elf asked the queen to come and see the daisies when they shut themselves up in the evening time.

'Oh, Pippitty!' she said. 'They're all tipped with pink! How beautiful! You're *quite* forgiven for all your naughtiness, and this can be your work now, always and always.'

'I'll love it,' said Pippitty, feeling as happy as a lark, 'and I'll never play naughty tricks again, Your Majesty.'

And if you look at the daisies when they close themselves at night, you are sure to see some with pink tips – and you'll know the Pippitty Elf has been along there with his precious pink paint and little pointed paint brush.

Mr Twiddle
and the Cat

Mr Twiddle and the Cat

MR TWIDDLE had a cold. He sneezed and snuffled, and Mrs Twiddle was very sorry for him.

'You shall have a hot drink,' she said, 'and I will buy you some nice lozenges to suck. Now, just sit by the fire, Twiddle, and keep warm.'

Twiddle sat by the fire and toasted his legs and knees. The cat came up and purred. It loved a warm fire as much as Mr Twiddle did.

Puss jumped up on to Mr Twiddle's knee, and dug a claw into his trousers to hold on by. Twiddle gave a yell!

'Ow! You tiresome cat! You've pricked me with

your claw. Get down! I've enough to do with warming myself without having you on my knee too!'

He pushed the cat down. Puss waited a few minutes till Mr Twiddle shut his eyes and nodded – and then up jumped Puss again. Mr Twiddle got a shock. His pipe fell out of his mouth and broke on the hearth.

He was very angry. 'Look at that!' he said to the cat. 'Look what you've done, you careless animal!'

Now the more Twiddle lost his temper with the cat, the more Puss seemed to want to come to him. It was most annoying. First the cat lay down on his feet, and he had to shuffle it off. Then it jumped up on to the back of his chair and tried to lie round his neck. That made him very angry.

'Are you trying to be a scarf or something?' said Mr Twiddle to the cat. 'Get down! I don't want you on my feet and I don't want you round my neck. You are a real nuisance tonight. Do leave me alone.'

The cat disappeared. Mr Twiddle went to sleep. When he woke up he wanted to read the newspaper, so up he got to fetch it. He didn't see the cat lying on the rug, curled up in a ball. He trod on it, fell flat on his nose, and the cat leapt up and scratched his cheek. Dear me, what an upset there was! Mr Twiddle yelled, the cat yowled and spat, and Mrs Twiddle came running in to see what the matter was.

'Twiddle, how dare you be unkind to the cat!' she cried. Twiddle got up and glared at her.

'You just scold the cat, not me,' he said. 'It's she who is being unkind to *me*! She won't leave me alone!'

He felt for his glasses. They had fallen off his nose. Mr Twiddle went down on his hands and knees to find them. He put his hand under the sofa, but the cat was hiding there, and thought he was playing. So she patted his fingers, and made him jump.

'If that cat isn't under the sofa now!' said Mr Twiddle. 'Wife, I tell you she won't leave me alone! Take her away. I can't bear any more tonight.'

Mrs Twiddle took the cat into the scullery and shut the door on her. The cat jumped up on to the table, found Mr Twiddle's supper there, ready for cooking, and ate it all up. Dear me, how angry he was when he heard about it!

'I'm going to bed,' he said. 'I can't stand that cat any more. There's something strange about it tonight. It just won't leave me alone.'

'Don't be silly, Twiddle,' said his wife. She got up and went into the scullery. She filled a hot-water bottle and put a nice, warm, furry cover on it. Then she went upstairs to put it into Twiddle's bed, while he went round the house and locked the doors.

Twiddle undressed. He grinned to himself when he thought of how he had shooed the cat out of the back door into the dark night. Now it wouldn't bother him any more. Ha, ha! He wouldn't tell Mrs Twiddle. She would be cross if she knew the cat was out at night.

He threw back the sheets and jumped into bed. He put his feet down – and good gracious me, whatever was that in the bed? Twiddle gave a loud yell, jumped out again, and glared fearfully at the lump in the bed.

'That cat again!' he said. 'How did it get there? No sooner did I put my feet down than I felt it, all warm and furry. It's a magic cat tonight. What am I to do? I simply don't dare to get into bed. I shan't tell Mrs Twiddle. She will only laugh at me.'

Mrs Twiddle was sleeping in the spare room bed that night, because she didn't want to catch Twiddle's cold. Her light was out. Twiddle stood in his bedroom and shivered.

'Fancy that tiresome cat thinking it would sleep in my bed!' he said to himself. 'Whatever next? And I shooed it out of the back door too! Well, I shall put on my dressing gown and spend the night in my chair in front of the kitchen fire. If that cat thinks it's going to bite my toes all night, it's mistaken!'

Poor Twiddle! He went downstairs and settled himself by the fire. He was almost asleep when Mrs Twiddle appeared, looking most surprised.

'Twiddle! Whatever are you doing? I looked

in your room to see if you were all right, and you weren't there!'

'I couldn't get into bed,' said Twiddle sulkily. 'That cat was there.'

'Don't be silly, Twiddle. She never goes upstairs,' said Mrs Twiddle.

'I'm not silly,' said Twiddle. 'I tell you, that cat is lying in my bed, and I'm not going to sleep with it.'

Just then there came a mewing outside the back door, and something scratched and scraped at the door.

'But *that's* the cat!' cried Mrs Twiddle in surprise. 'I'd know her mew anywhere! However is it that she's outside, poor darling?'

'That's not the cat,' said Twiddle. 'I tell you, she's upstairs in my bed, as warm as a pie.'

Mrs Twiddle opened the back door – and in bounded the cat, purring with delight. She jumped straight on to Twiddle's knee. He gave a yell.

'Get off! Wife, there must be two cats then. I tell you one is asleep in my bed.'

'Well, we'll come and see,' said Mrs Twiddle, thinking that Twiddle must be quite mad. They went upstairs, and Mrs Twiddle threw back the covers. In the middle of the bed was the hot-water bottle she had put there, warm and cosy in its furry cover!

'You thought your hot-water bottle was the c-c-c-cat!' cried Mrs Twiddle, beginning to laugh and laugh. 'And you went downstairs in a rage, and left your lovely hot bottle to sleep in the bed by itself! Oh, Twiddle! Oh, Twiddle, you'll make me die of laughing one of these days!'

She laughed till she cried. Twiddle was angry and ashamed. He got into bed, put his feet on the hot bottle, and covered himself up.

'I'll have no more to do with that cat from now on,' he said. But, dear me, as soon as he was asleep, Puss jumped up on his bed and slept peacefully on Twiddle's feet all night long. Wouldn't Twiddle have been cross if he'd known!

Snifty's Lamppost

Snifty's Lamppost

ONCE UPON a time there lived a very disagreeable gnome called Snifty. He was head of the gnome village he lived in, and he was very unkind to everyone.

Now, the chancellor of Gnomeland came to visit him one night. There was no moon, and it was so dark that the chancellor could hardly see his way through the village. He drove down the wrong path, and when he got out of his carriage to see where he was, he fell over two or three geese and then sat down on a frightened pig.

This made him very cross, and when he got to Snifty's house he told him that he ought to be ashamed of having a village which was so dreadfully dark.

'Why don't you have a new lamppost put just in front of your house?' he asked. 'Then your visitors would know where you lived, and would not fall over pigs and geese.'

'I will,' said Snifty, rubbing his hands gleefully, glad to think that his villagers would have to buy a fine lamppost for him out of their own money. He didn't once think of buying it himself. He always made his poor people pay for everything, and because they were afraid of him, they did not dare to say no.

So the next day he sent a notice round the village to say that the gnomes were to make him a fine new lamppost. Then when the chancellor visited him another night he wouldn't go the wrong way.

'Will you give us the money for it?' asked the gnomes.

'Certainly not!' answered Snifty. 'What is the use of being the chief if I can't get things for nothing, I should like to know?'

The gnomes knew that it was of no use to say anything more, but they were very angry.

'It's time we made Snifty stop this sort of thing,' they grumbled. 'He's always expecting us to pay for everything, and he never gives us a penny towards it.'

They began to make the lamppost. It was a lovely one, for the gnomes liked making things as beautifully as they could, no matter whether they were working for people they liked or disliked.

Snifty soon sent them word that the chancellor was coming to see him again, and he ordered the gnomes to have the lamppost put up in time.

Then the gnomes grumbled even more, and suddenly they decided that they would do just what Snifty said, and no more. They would finish the lamppost and put it up – but they wouldn't put any oil in the lamp, or light it! That would just serve old Snifty right!

So they finished the lamppost and put it up just in front of Snifty's front gate. He watched them from the window, but he didn't bother to come out and say thank you.

The chancellor arrived that evening, and again it was very, very dark. No one had put any oil in the lamp or lit it, so there was no light for him to see by again. He was very cross, especially when his carriage got stuck in the ditch and couldn't be moved. He got out and trod on a hedgehog, which hurt him very much.

'Why doesn't Snifty do as I tell him, and get a lamppost put in front of his gate?' he growled. 'He's rich enough!'

Snifty was very angry when he found that the lamp was not lit. The chancellor told him how his carriage had stuck in the ditch, and asked him why it was that he had not got his lamp lit to show him the way. Snifty rang a bell, and told his servant to fetch some of the village gnomes, and he would hear why they had disobeyed him.

The gnomes soon came, and Snifty asked them angrily why they had not obeyed him.

'We have obeyed you, sir,' answered the gnomes. 'You told us to put a lamppost in front of your gate, and we have done so. But you did not tell us to put any oil in it.'

'Oh, you silly, foolish creatures!' cried Snifty angrily. 'Then hear me now. The chancellor is coming again tomorrow night, and oil is to be put in the lamp. Do you hear?'

'Yes,' said the gnomes, and went out.

When they had got to their homes they put their heads together and decided that they would again do exactly as Snifty had said – they would put oil in the lamp, but no wick!

So next day oil was poured into the lamp, but no wick was put in. And when the chancellor arrived that night he again found that he could not see where Snifty lived! This time he jumped out of his carriage too soon, and walked straight into a very muddy pond. He was so angry when he reached Snifty's at last that he could hardly speak.

Once again Snifty called the gnomes to his house, and asked them what they meant by not obeying him.

'Sir, we have obeyed you,' answered the gnomes. 'We have put oil in the lamp as you bade us. You did not tell us to put in a wick – so how could the lamp be lit?'

'Then put in a wick!' shouted Snifty, very angry indeed.

So next day the gnomes put a fine big wick into the lamp, but they did not light it.

'Snifty said "put in a wick" – he did not say light the wick,' said the gnomes, grinning among themselves.

This time the chancellor was so certain that the lamp would be alight that he drove right through the village without seeing it, looking all the time for Snifty's lit lamp. When he stopped and asked where he was, he found that he had driven three miles beyond the village. So he had to turn his carriage round and go back.

'Are you disobeying me on purpose?' he asked

Snifty, when he at last arrived. 'Where is that lamp?'

'Isn't it lit?' cried Snifty.

'No, it isn't,' answered the chancellor.

'Then I'll find out why!' cried Snifty in a rage, and he called in the gnomes once more.

'Why have you disobeyed me again?' he shouted angrily.

'We have not disobeyed you!' answered the gnomes in surprise. 'You told us to put a wick in the lamp, and we have done so. We did not hear you order us to light the wick.'

'Then tomorrow light the wick!' roared Snifty.

The gnomes consulted among themselves, and decided that the next night they would light the wick as Snifty had commanded, and then blow it out! So they would be obeying him, and yet he still would not have his light.

They did this. One of them lit the lamp carefully, and then after five minutes he blew the light out. Then they waited for the chancellor to come as usual.

This time the chancellor was so angry to find that the lamp was again not lit for him that he almost deafened Snifty with his shouting. Snifty called in the gnomes again, and they explained that he had told them to light the lamp, and they had done so. He had not told them to let it burn all night long, and as oil was expensive they had blown out the light after five minutes.

Snifty was too furious to speak for a whole minute.

'Tomorrow you will light the wick which rests in the oil, and you will see that the lamp is burning all night long,' he cried at last. 'I will have no misunderstanding this time.'

The gnomes went away. For some time they could not think of any way in which they might again trick Snifty, and yet still obey him. Then one of them had a good idea.

'Snifty didn't say anything about where the lamp was to be, did he?' he said. 'Let's move it away from his gate when night comes, and put it somewhere else.

We'll light it, and keep it burning all night long – but it won't be in the right place!'

The other gnomes thought this was a splendid idea. So when night came, they went quietly to where the lamppost was and carried it away to the other end of the village, and there they lit it.

Very soon the chancellor came by, and seeing the light, he stopped and got out of his carriage. He was very much puzzled when he could see no sign of Snifty's house. He stopped a little gnome and asked him.

'Oh, Snifty lives at the other end of the village,' answered the gnome.

'Oh, dear, oh, dear!' said the chancellor. 'What a nuisance! I have got the king of Gnomeland in my carriage tonight, and I didn't want to lose my way as I usually do. I told Snifty to be sure and have the lamp alight outside his front gate, so that I would know where I was.'

Now when the little gnome heard that the king was

in the carriage, he was very much surprised. He told the other gnomes, and very quickly they lifted up the lamppost and carried it in front of the carriage to show the driver the way. They set the lamp down by Snifty's front gates, and then cheered the king loudly as he drove by.

'What very nice, good-natured fellows,' said the king, pleased. 'Snifty is lucky to have such fine people in his village.'

When they reached the house, the chancellor told Snifty that again there had been no lamp outside his house, and sternly asked him why. Snifty gasped with rage and called in his gnomes at once.

'Why have you disobeyed me again?' he cried.

'We haven't disobeyed you,' answered the gnomes. 'You told us to light the lamp, and keep it burning all night long. But you didn't say it was to be outside your gates.'

Then Snifty lost his temper and said some rude and horrid things to the gnomes in front of the king.

The king stopped him and asked to be told the tale. When he found that night after night Snifty had been tricked over the lamp, he was very much puzzled.

'But your villagers seem such good-natured fellows,' he said. 'Why, they carried the lamp all the way in front of my carriage for me! It is very wrong of them to behave like this. After all, it is your lamp, for you have paid for it, Snifty. They have no right to treat it like that.'

'Excuse me, Your Majesty,' said a gnome, stepping forward. 'We had to pay for the lamp, not Snifty. He makes us pay for everything he wants. If he had paid for the lamp himself, we should not have tried to teach him a lesson.'

'Are you poor?' the king asked Snifty.

'No, Your Majesty,' said Snifty, beginning to tremble.

'Then why do you not pay for your lamp yourself?' asked the king. 'Many tales have reached me lately, Snifty, of your meanness, and I came here to find out if they were true or not. I now see very plainly that they are. Your people were quite right to treat you as you deserve. You must leave the village, and I will make someone else the chief!'

So Snifty had to go, and you may be sure nobody missed him. As for the lamp, it now burns brightly outside the new chief's gates every night and reminds him to be kind and generous. If he isn't, I don't know what trick the gnomes would play on him – but I'm sure they would think of something!

The Foolish Green Frog

The Foolish Green Frog

THERE WAS once a green frog who used to float in Peter's bath every night. He was a nice little toy frog, and he and the toy goldfish swam together for Peter and made him laugh.

One day, Peter took the toy frog out into the garden with him. He played with it for a little while and then he threw it on to the grass. When it began to rain he ran indoors and left the frog by itself.

The frog didn't like the rain. It was afraid its nice green paint would come off. So it hopped away under a bush. And there it met a big thrush, turning over some moss to hunt for snails.

'Hallo!' said the thrush in surprise. 'What are you doing here, little frog? I thought all good frogs lived in ponds in the springtime.'

'Is that so?' said the little frog. 'Well, I will certainly go to live in the pond too.'

'Shall I show you the way?' asked the thrush politely. 'You are not very big so perhaps you are not old enough to know the way.'

'I can find it by myself, thank you,' said the frog haughtily. 'I am quite big enough. Goodbye!'

He hopped off to look for the pond. He longed to be a proper frog and not a toy one. He wanted to play with other frogs and have a good time.

But he didn't really know what the pond was like, so after a bit, when he met a garden snail he stopped and spoke to him.

'Good day,' he said, 'could you tell me if I am anywhere near the pond?'

'Well,' said the snail, looking all around, 'that looks like it over there, doesn't it!'

The snail pointed with his horns to a large puddle on the path. The snail was very small so to him the puddle was as large as a pond. The frog took his word for it and at once leapt over to the puddle. He lay down in it, hoping that very soon he would see one or two real frogs to play with. But he didn't.

The sun came out and shone warmly, and very soon the puddle began to dry up! Then the frog found himself lying on a dry path, and the thrush, who came flying by at that moment, laughed loudly.

'Did you think that puddle was the pond?' he cried. 'Oh, you funny little fellow! That was only a puddle, and now it is dried up, so if you don't move someone will come along and tread on you!'

The frog hopped off quickly, angry with the laughing thrush. Soon he came to a big old sink, lying on the ground full of water. The gardener had put it there for the hens to drink from, but the little frog felt sure it was a pond. So into the old sink it hopped and swam around looking for more frogs to play with. But he didn't find any.

Soon, along came two big hens to have a drink, and they clucked loudly when they saw the little green frog.

'A frog in the drinking water! Think of that! Let's drink him up!'

They pecked at the frightened frog, but he sprang out of the old sink and hopped away. One hen poked him with her beak and made a dent in his shoulder. He didn't like it at all.

On and on he went, and at last came to a big rain barrel into which dripped water from the roofs. Beside it was a worm, poking his head out of a hole.

'Good day,' said the frog. 'Can you tell me where the pond is?'

'What is a pond?' asked the worm in wonder, for he had never left his little hole in all his life.

'Oh, it's a lot of water,' said the frog.

'Dear me, then that must be the pond in this great barrel you see,' said the worm. 'I once heard the robin say that it was full of water.'

'Thank you,' said the frog, and you should have seen him making his way up the side of the barrel! It was quite exciting to watch him, and the worm felt certain he would tumble off and bump his head on the ground. But he didn't. He reached the top in safety and dived into the water that filled the barrel.

There were no other frogs there. It was most disappointing. The little toy frog swam about and then he suddenly saw a big face looking at him. It was the cook, coming out to get a pail full of water from the rain barrel, and she *was* surprised to see a frog there!

He was so frightened that he leapt straight out of the rain tub and fell to the ground.

'What are you doing in our rain barrel?' cried the cook. Then he knew that he hadn't been in the pond after all. On he went again – and at last he really did come to the pond!

But it wasn't the frog pond – no it was the duck pond! No frogs live in duck ponds for the ducks eat every one that they find. But the little toy frog didn't know that. He was so anxious to be a real, proper frog that he didn't think of any danger, but jumped head first into the duck pond and swam about to find some friends to play with.

But the only creatures there were the big white ducks! They saw him, and thinking he was a real live frog, they all came swimming up.

'Here's a frog!' they quacked. 'Here's a frog! Let's eat him! Oh, what a fine morsel!'

The frog was frightened almost out of his wits! He must run away quickly before these big white birds pecked him and swallowed him. Out of the pond he jumped and all the ducks waddled out of the water after him.

Then suddenly something swooped down on him from the air and snapped him up – and off he went into the air to the sound of flapping wings! At first he thought the duck had caught him, but soon he heard a chuckle and knew that it was the thrush who had offered so politely to show him the way to the pond.

'Well,' said the thrush, 'you've made a pretty mess of things, haven't you? I've watched you, and how I've laughed! I saw you in a puddle, and I saw you nearly drunk by those hens. I watched you climb into the rain tub and how I chuckled when you sprang into the duck pond! I was just in time to rescue you!'

'Oh, thank you,' said the little green frog gratefully. 'I'm sorry I was rude to you at first. Where are you taking me to?'

'Well, don't you want to go to the frog pond?' asked the thrush.

'Not now,' said the frog. 'I've learnt my lesson. I'm not a real frog and I never will be. I'm only a toy frog and I'd better try to be what I'm meant to be – something for a little boy to play with. Will you take me back to Peter?'

'You'll just be in time for his bath!' said the thrush. He flew in at the open window and dropped the frog from his beak. Splash! He fell into a bath of warm water, and a little voice cried out, 'Oh, look! Here's Froggy back again! Oh, wherever did he come from?'

It was Peter, having a bath! He *was* so pleased to see the little frog, and as for the toy goldfish he nearly went mad with joy to see his friend once more.

I shall never try to be grand. again, thought the toy frog, swimming happily in the bath. And as far as I know, he swims each night there still!

The Little Paper Boats

The Little Paper Boats

ONE NIGHT, when Paul and Mary were fast asleep, someone came knocking at their bedroom window.

'Tap!' went the noise. 'Tap-tap! Tap!'

Mary woke up first and thought it was the wind blowing a branch against the window. Then she thought it wasn't, because it did sound so exactly like someone knocking. So she woke Paul up.

'Doesn't it sound as if someone is outside?' she whispered. 'Do you suppose it is a pixie?'

'Let's look!' said Paul and he jumped out of bed to see. The moon shone brightly outside – and what *do* you think he saw? Standing on the windowsill was a tiny creature dressed in silver, and she was tapping with her hand on the pane. 'Tap-tap! Tap!'

'It *is* a pixie or an elf!' cried Paul in delight. He opened the window and the tiny creature climbed in.

'Oh, do forgive my waking you,' she said. 'But a dreadful thing has happened.'

'What?' cried both children.

'Well, you know the stream that runs to the bottom of your garden?' said the pixie. 'We were going to meet the fairy queen on the opposite side tonight, because she is going to hold a meeting there – and we had our pixie ship all ready to take us across. But a big wind blew suddenly and broke the rope that tied our ship to the shore. So now we can't get across because the ship has floated away, and we *are* so upset.'

'Oh, what a pity!' said Mary. 'Can we help you?'

'That's what I came to ask you,' said the pixie. 'Could you lend us a toy boat to sail across in?'

'We did have one,' said Paul, 'but it's broken. Its sail is gone, and it floats all on one side. I'm afraid it wouldn't be a bit of use to you.'

'Oh, dear!' said the pixie, looking ready to burst into tears. 'Isn't that too bad? We felt quite sure you would have one. Have you anything else that would do?'

'No, I'm afraid not,' said Paul, trying to think of something. 'We've no raft, and not even a little penny rowing boat. I *am* sorry!'

'Well, never mind,' said the pixie, climbing out to the windowsill. 'We shall just have to stay on this side of the stream and hope that the queen will not be too cross with us. We have no wings, you see, or we could fly across.'

Mary suddenly clapped her hands. 'I know!' she cried. 'I know! What about some paper boats, pixie? Paul and I can make nice paper boats that will float on the water. They don't last very long but they would take you across the stream all right, I'm sure. Shall we make you some?'

'Oh, will you?' asked the pixie in delight. 'That *is*

kind of you! Thank you so much!'

'That's a good idea of yours, Mary,' said Paul. 'Quick, let's put on our dressing gowns and go down to the stream with the pixie. We can take a newspaper with us and make as many boats as they like.'

So they put on their dressing gowns, took an old newspaper from the cupboard, and then ran downstairs and out into the garden. The pixie met them there and they all three went down to the little stream that ran at the foot of the garden.

What a sight the two children saw! The moon shone brightly down on a crowd of little silvery creatures, dressed in misty gowns. They had tiny pointed faces and little high voices like swallows twittering. They were astonished to see the children and ran helter-skelter to hide. But the pixie that came with Paul and Mary called them back.

'It's quite safe,' she cried. 'These children are going to help us. They will make us some boats.'

'A small boat will take one or two of you,' said

Paul. 'We'll make some of all sizes – and then some of you can go in crowds and some can go in twos and threes, just as you like.'

He and Mary began to tear the paper into oblongs, and then, very quickly, they folded their paper into this shape and that, until at last there came a little paper boat. The pixies watched them in delight. They had never seen such a thing before.

Paul and Mary soon put two boats on the water, and two or three pixies clambered in. The boat went rocking up and down on the stream, and the pixie guided it towards the opposite bank. They screamed with delight as it went, and all the pixies left on shore begged Paul and Mary to hurry up and make some more boats for them. Very soon there was a whole fleet of the little paper boats on the stream and the pixies sprang into them in joy. Across to the opposite shore they sailed one by one and landed safely on the opposite side.

The last pixie left was the one who had tapped on

the bedroom window. Mary made her a dear little boat for herself and the pixie stepped into it.

'Goodbye,' she said. 'Don't wait here any longer, in case you catch cold. It's been so kind of you to help us. If you find our ship you may keep it for your own. It's a dear little ship, and we'd like you to have it.'

The children waved goodbye and then went indoors to bed, talking excitedly of all that had happened. They thought that they were much too excited to go to sleep, but it wasn't long before they were dreaming, their heads cuddled into their pillows.

The next day they were quite certain they had dreamt it all, and they were surprised to find that they had both had the same dream – but they really didn't think they *could* have seen pixies in the night. It didn't seem real in the morning.

But what do you think they found later on in the day, when they went for a walk down by their stream? The little ship belonging to the pixies! There it was, caught in some rushes, a little silver-sailed ship with the name *Silver Pixie* on its hull! Then they knew that their dream was true, and in great delight they rushed home to show their mother what they had found.

They keep the ship on the nursery mantelpiece because it is so pretty – and there it is to this day, a little, glittering, silver ship! It sails beautifully, and you should see all the children stare when Paul and Mary take it down to the pond to sail!

I'd love to see it, wouldn't you?

The Little Clockwork Mouse

The Little Clockwork Mouse

THE CLOCKWORK mouse peeped out of the brick box. He liked to live there because he could get under the bricks when he wanted to hide. No one was about. The mouse crept out and ran over the floor just like a real mouse.

He peeped inside the doll's house. He saw everything ready there for a party. Little Mrs Doll, who lived there, was giving it that night at twelve o'clock. She had invited all the tiny toys, the ones that could get easily inside the house. Teddy and the big dolls were not invited. The doll's house was not very large, and if the big toys came to the party there was no room to play games or to dance.

So little Mrs Doll had only asked Belinda, the small girl doll; Piggy, who wasn't much bigger than himself; the yellow duck from the toy farmyard; and the two cats from the Noah's Ark.

But she hadn't asked the clockwork mouse. This was a pity, the little mouse thought, for he was quite small enough to get easily into the doll's house, and he did so like a party. He was very sad about it. He had thought Mrs Doll liked him, but now he was afraid that she didn't, and he tried to think why.

I always say good morning to her when I meet her, he thought. *I always woffle my nose most politely at her when she smiles at me. I run errands for her when she asks me. I can't think what I have done to upset her. Well, well, it's a sad thing not to be asked to somebody's party and not know why.*

The doll's house looked very pretty, for the table was set for the party and there were small balloons hanging down from the ceiling. The floor had been polished for dancing and shone brightly. In the kitchen there were some lemons all ready to be cut up for lemonade. The clockwork mouse could smell them. He liked lemonade.

Mrs Doll was upstairs in the bedroom dressing the two children dolls. She was talking to them as she brushed their hair.

'Everything is ready,' she said, 'and it looks very nice indeed. But I do wish I had some flowers to put about the rooms. That's the worst of a doll's house – there is never any garden, so I've no flowers to pick. A house doesn't look right without flowers. But I haven't got any, so it's no use grumbling about it.'

Now, when the clockwork mouse heard this, he pricked up his small ears. Flowers! He knew where there were some flowers! There were a great many daisies outside the window, growing in the grass. They were small flowers, just right for a doll's house. He would go and pick some and put them in the vases for Mrs Doll and give her a nice surprise. He wouldn't tell her who had done it, in case she was feeling cross with him about something – he would just do it.

He ran over to the big teddy bear.

'Would you mind winding me up till you can't wind me any more?' he asked. 'I want to go out into the garden, and I don't want my clockwork to run down before I get back.'

Clickity-clickity-clickity-click! The teddy bear wound the mouse's key round and round and round in his side. He went on till he could wind no more. The mouse was wound up as much as he could possibly be.

'Thank you, Teddy,' he said, and ran off. He went to a mouse hole he knew, down which lived a real mouse, and made his way along the little mouse passage and out of a hole in the wall, leading to the garden.

There were lots of daisies in the grass. The mouse chose the smallest and nibbled the stalks in two to pick them, because his paws were not made so that he could pick them properly. He could not carry them in his paws either, for he had to run on those, so he laid each daisy down as he picked it. Then, when he had enough, he picked up the little bunch in his mouth and ran back through the mouse hole.

He crept up to the doll's house and listened. Mrs Doll was still upstairs, getting ready. The little mouse ran in and took four vases – one from the table, one from the mantelpiece, one from the sideboard and one from the bookcase. He went to the kitchen and turned on the tiny tap. He filled each little vase with water. Then he put them on the kitchen table and carefully placed each daisy in water with his mouth. Three daisies were enough for each vase. The daisies were very pretty, because they were pink-tipped.

The mouse carried each vase carefully into the dining room, and set them out. How lovely they looked! Mrs Doll would be most surprised. He heard her coming downstairs, so he raced out of the house and went back to his brick box and listened for sounds of the party.

Mrs Doll went into the dining room to see that everything was ready, and she saw the four vases of flowers so neatly arranged – one on the mantelpiece, one on the table, one on the sideboard and one on the bookcase. She stared in surprise and delight.

'Who has done this?' she cried. 'Oh, it's just what I wanted to make the party quite perfect!'

But nobody knew who had done it. Soon the guests began to arrive. Belinda Doll came first, wearing her new blue silk frock, pink sash and tiny shoes. Then came Piggy, tripping along on his pink feet, grunting happily. Then the yellow duck from the farmyard waddled up to the party, and quacked loudly when she saw such a fine feast set ready.

Mrs Doll waited and waited for the two cats to come from the Noah's Ark. But they didn't come. At last the brown bear from the Noah's Ark came running up to say that the cats were very sorry, but somehow they had got shut into one of the carriages of the toy train and nobody could open the door to get them out. So they wouldn't be able to come.

'There now!' said Mrs Doll, vexed. 'We are two short. Well, Bear, you had better stay to the party. And we want one more.'

'Where's the clockwork mouse?' said the Noah's Ark bear, looking round. 'I saw him popping in here this evening with a whole lot of daisies in his mouth, so I thought you must have asked him to the party, but I don't see him anywhere!'

'You saw him with the daisies!' cried Mrs Doll. 'So that's where the flowers came from. How nice of the little creature to give me flowers when he hadn't been asked to the party! Belinda Doll, go and ask him to come. He lives in the brick box.'

Belinda Doll ran off to the brick box and saw the clockwork mouse peeping at her. 'You're to come to the party, Mouse,' she said. 'Hurry up!'

'But I haven't any party clothes ready,' said the mouse.

'Well, here's a pink ribbon to tie round your neck,'

said kind Belinda Doll. She undid her sash and gave it to the mouse. She tied it neatly round his neck and fluffed out the bow. 'Now you look beautiful,' she said.

They went to the doll's house together. Mrs Doll gave the clockwork mouse a hug. 'I'm so pleased to see you!' she said. 'It was very, very kind of you to bring me these lovely flowers for my party, especially when you had been left out.'

'Well, I did just wonder why you left me out,' said the mouse.

'Oh, I only left you out because I thought the two cats from the Noah's Ark were coming,' said Mrs Doll. 'And I was just a bit afraid they might chase you, as you are a mouse. I didn't want you to be frightened, you see. But now that the two cats are not coming, there is no reason why you should not come to the party too!'

'Hurrah!' cried the mouse, running round and round after his own tail. 'I'm glad I was nice about it and picked you some flowers, instead of sulking and thinking horrid things. Hurrah! I do love a party!'

They did have a good time. They danced, and they played musical chairs and blindman's buff, and they ate jellies and buns and sweets, and drank lemonade; and the clockwork mouse tied a balloon to Piggy's tail and made everyone laugh!

'It's been the loveliest party!' said the clockwork mouse when he said goodnight. 'Thank you very much!' Then back he ran to the brick box and fell fast asleep.

Mr Dozey's Dream

Mr Dozey's Dream

MR DOZEY lived just outside Tiptop Village in a dirty little tumbledown cottage. He was a lazy fellow who never did a day's work if he could help it.

One day he had a very pleasant surprise. Mr and Mrs Tuck-In were giving a party, and they asked everyone in the village, even old Mr Dozey! The postman put his invitation through his letterbox, and he was most surprised when he opened it.

'A party! I haven't been to one for years,' said Dozey. 'The thing is, what am I to wear? I want a new coat and waistcoat and a new pair of trousers and a hat and pair of shoes. Can I borrow them from anyone?'

But nobody would lend old Dozey anything. They had got tired of that years ago. Whatever they lent Dozey never came back!

Everyone said the same thing to him when he came asking for clothes for the party. 'Dozey, you go and do what everyone else does, you work a bit, and earn some money to buy your own clothes!'

Dozey was annoyed. 'How mean they are!' he said to Blinks, his cat. 'Not a scrap of kindness in them. Well, I've a good mind to go along to Ma Shuffle and borrow a spell. If she'd give me a change-a-bit spell, I could use it on my old clothes, and change them into new ones.' This seemed a very good idea indeed to Dozey. He appeared at Ma's door, and smiled and bowed.

'What do you want?' said Ma briskly. 'Come to ask for a job of work? Well, you go into my garden and do a bit of weeding, and you might sweep the path while you're about it, and there's a corner over there that wants digging, and . . .'

Dozey was horrified. What, do all that work! What was Ma thinking of?

'I came to borrow a change-a-bit spell,' he said. 'I want to change these old clothes of mine into nice ones for the party.'

'The only reason I'd lend you a change-a-bit spell is to change you from a lazy, sly old fellow into a hard-working, decent one,' said Ma sharply. 'If you want new clothes, earn them. Get along now! I'm expecting a visitor, my brother, Mr Rumbustious. He'll soon send you packing if you're round here when he comes.'

Dozey didn't like Mr Rumbustious, so he walked off, annoyed. He went through the woods, muttering to himself.

It was a very hot day, and Dozey soon felt tired. He sat down under a bush and went to sleep. He dreamt a wonderful dream. In his dream he had a marvellous new suit of clothes, from a hat with a feather in, to a blue silk waistcoat and shoes to match.

And would you believe it, when he awoke, the very first thing he saw hanging on a tree nearby was a fine suit of clothes, with a feathered hat, a shirt, waistcoat, trousers, shoes and coat! Dozey was too astonished for words.

'My word! Look at that! My dream's come true. I'm a lucky fellow today, no doubt about that! Ha! I'll dress myself in these and then go and show myself to old Ma Shuffle!'

So he took off his own things and threw them down. He dressed himself in the smart new suit of clothes and felt very grand indeed.

He strode to the nearby pond and looked at himself in the clear water. 'Sir Magnificent Dozey!' he said, and bowed to his own reflection. Then he thought he would go and parade up and down the village street and let everyone see him and admire him.

Off he went, the feather waving in his hat. It was a pity he hadn't washed himself in the pool, and it was a pity too that he hadn't combed his hair that morning!

Everyone stopped and stared at this well-dressed Dozey, as he paraded up and down, nodding and bowing.

'Where did you get those clothes, Mr Dozey?' asked little Button in surprise.

'I dreamt them and they came true!' said Dozey grandly.

'A very useful sort of dream,' said Button disbelievingly, and ran off.

After he had shown himself off for half an hour, Dozey went to Ma Shuffle's. Ho, wouldn't she stare! He wondered if her brother Mr Rumbustious was there yet. He didn't like him at all, too noisy and very rude at times to people like Dozey. Well, Dozey was certain that Mr Rumbustious had never in his life been clever enough to dream a dream that immediately came true!

Dozey thought he would peep in at the window of Ma's cottage to see if Rumbustious had arrived yet. So he went round into the garden, and was just about to peep through the window when he heard Mr Rumbustious's enormous voice booming away inside.

'I tell you, Ma, if I get hold of that fellow I'll throw him up to the moon! The thief! The robber! The mean, sneaking fellow!'

'Well, Rumbustious,' began Ma's voice, but her brother interrupted again immediately.

'I was walking through the woods, and I was hot. I came to the pool – it looked so clear and cool. So I pulled my clothes off – my best ones, mind – and into the pool I went. And I tell you, Ma, when I came out my clothes had gone – yes, even my new feathered hat – and these filthy rags were left instead. *Gr-r-r!* If I get hold of that fellow, I'll throw him up to—'

'Yes. You said that before, Rumbustious,' said Ma. 'But let's think – who in the world could it have been? Who would dare to do a thing like that? He would have to walk away in your grand clothes and everyone would see him!'

Outside the window Dozey's knees began to

knock together. His face went pale. He felt very peculiar indeed.

His dream hadn't come true! Mr Rumbustious had come along while he had been dozing, hadn't seen him and had undressed and gone for a swim – and while he was in the water, he, Dozey, had woken up and dressed in Mr Rumbustious's clothes. Whatever was he to do now?

'I tell you, if I catch that fellow, I'll throw . . .' began Rumbustious again, in his enormous voice. That was too much for poor Dozey. He ran to the gate, and little Shuffle saw him from the door!

'Ma! There's the thief – Mr Dozey! He's got all Uncle's clothes on!' cried Shuffle, and out he went with Mr Rumbustious to catch Dozey.

Well, Mr Dozey's knees were still knocking together, so he couldn't run very fast, and very soon he was being marched into Ma's kitchen by Shuffle and his uncle.

'I can explain it to Mr Plod the village policeman,'

said Rumbustious. 'And after that I'm going to throw you up to—'

'No, no, no!' cried Dozey in fright. He turned to Ma Shuffle. 'Ma, save me! It was all a mistake! What can I do to show you it was?'

'Oh, well, now you're talking sense,' said Ma. 'Didn't I tell you this very morning there was some weeding to do, and the path to be swept, and a corner that wants digging, and . . .'

And that's how it came about that Mr Dozey spent three whole days working hard in Ma Shuffle's garden, with little Shuffle keeping an eye on him through the window. He's not going to the party though – no, he doesn't like meeting anyone just now. They all said the same thing:

'Hi, Dozey! Any more dreams come true?'

You Help Me, and I'll Help You

You Help Me, and I'll Help You

JIMBO WAS a beautiful Siamese cat. His coat was brown and cream, his paws were brown, and so were his ears and his face. But his eyes were as blue as the summer sky.

He had a lovely big garden to play in, but he loved to wander in the fields and the woods nearby. He liked to lie in wait for the rabbits, though he never managed to catch even a baby one, because they were all much too quick for him.

'It's really annoying, the way they all pop down holes as soon as I begin to chase them,' said Jimbo, with a loud miaow. 'I wonder if I could get down a rabbit hole?'

Well, he tried one day, but a little way down he came to a big rabbit. The rabbit glared at him, turned himself round at once and kicked out at Jimbo with his strong hind legs.

Biff! Biff! Poor Jimbo got such a bang on the nose that he shot halfway up the hole. He scrabbled out of it very quickly indeed.

I shan't go down a rabbit hole again, he thought, washing his nose very gently with his paw. *My goodness! That rabbit went off like a cannon. BIFF!*

Now one day as he was wandering through the wood, he scrambled through a bramble bush. Some of the thorns caught in his fur and tried to hold him. But he made his way through and came safely out of the prickly bush.

He ran on a few steps and then stopped. What was this pulling at him, scraping along the ground after him? He turned to see.

A dead bramble twig had caught hold of his fur and had held on round one leg. It was prickly and it hurt him. Jimbo sat down and tried to scrape the bramble spray off his back leg.

But it wouldn't move! All that happened was that the prickles pricked him harder. Jimbo mewed and ran on again, but it was no good – the bramble scraped behind him all the way and frightened him.

He fled up a tree and the bramble went with him. He rushed down and the bramble rushed down too. Wherever he went the prickly bramble twig held on tightly to him, and drove its prickles into his leg whenever he moved.

Jimbo sat down and howled.

'*Ow-ee-ow-ee-OW! Ow-ee-ow-ee-ow-ee-OW!*'

'Whatever is the matter?' said a small voice nearby. 'Do be quiet! You'll wake my baby!'

Jimbo stopped howling and looked round. He saw a very small pixie peering out of a hole in the bank. The hole was neatly covered by a pretty curtain of moss, and she was holding back the curtain and peering out.

Jimbo stared in surprise. It was the very first time

he had ever seen a pixie. Sometimes he had heard little pattering feet in the wood, and little high voices, but the pixies were very clever at disappearing as soon as he came near. Now here was one, with two tiny, pointed ears like a mouse, and two little eyes as green as the mossy curtain.

'You're sweet,' said Jimbo. 'Who are you?'

'I'm Tiptoe,' said the pixie. 'I live in this hole with Tiptap, my pixie husband. And we've got Tippy, the dearest little pixie baby you ever saw. You nearly woke him up with your dreadful yowls. What is the matter?'

'I'm sorry,' said Jimbo. 'But something has got hold of me and it's hurting me. Look!'

'Well! Whatever next? That's only a prickly bramble spray,' said Tiptoe, coming out of her little home. 'I can easily take that off for you!'

'Be careful you don't prick yourself,' said Jimbo. 'Ow! When you pulled, it hurt me! I got pricked!'

'Don't be such a silly,' said Tiptoe. 'You can't be

much more than a kitten if you make a fuss like that.'

'I'm not much more than a kitten,' said Jimbo. 'Oooh! Do be careful!'

'I can't pull carefully – the bramble is holding on too hard for that,' said Tiptoe. 'Now, just this last prickly bit and it will be all off!'

'Ooooh,' said Jimbo. 'That hurt too. Is it really gone? Oh, thank you! I'm sorry I nearly woke your baby. Can I see him?'

'Well – I'll hold this mossy curtain up and you can peep in if you like,' said Tiptoe. 'But you're far too big for even your whiskery face to go in. Just peep, that's all!'

So Jimbo peeped into the hole behind the curtain of moss. The dearest little home was there – a long, low room in the ground, hung with mossy curtains inside, and with a carpet of orange moss on the floor. Tiny furniture was there, made of twigs and leaves – and in a cradle slept the smallest creature Jimbo had ever seen – Tippy, the pixie's baby.

'I wish you could come in and have tea, but you can't,' said Tiptoe. 'Goodbye, now.'

'Tiptoe, perhaps I can do something for you, one day,' said Jimbo. 'You've helped me – and I'd love to help you.'

Tiptoe laughed. 'You won't be able to help me,' she said. 'Pixies don't ask cats for help. Do go, because you really will wake Tippy. Look – here is a tiny ball for you. Tippy has so many he'd love to give you one. You can play with it.'

She threw the tiny ball out of the hole and Jimbo bounded after it. It was hardly as big as a cherry, and just as red. He picked it up in his mouth proudly. He would keep it to remember Tippy by!

He hid it in his basket. Sometimes he sniffed at it and thought of Tiptoe and her kindness. He was afraid to go and see her again in case he woke the baby.

And then one night, when he was fast asleep in his basket on the veranda, someone came tugging at his fine whiskers. 'Wake up, Jimbo, do wake up. Quick,

Jimbo, WAKE UP!'

Jimbo woke up. The somebody pulled his whiskers again, and he mewed. 'Don't. Who is it?'

'It's me, Tiptoe! Jimbo, you once said you'd help me if you could. Well, will you?'

'Oh, Tiptoe! Is it really you?' cried Jimbo. 'And what's that you're holding? Your baby? What's happened?'

Tiptoe began to cry. 'Jimbo, it's the rat – the horrible, nasty, big brown rat! He came sniffing into our hole under the mossy curtain, and he turned me out, and Tiptap, my husband, out and the baby out too. All our lovely furniture is outside the hole as well. The rat says he wants the hole to live in. Oh, Jimbo!'

'Well! The very idea!' said Jimbo angrily. 'How dare a rat do something like that? I never heard of such a thing!'

'What can we do?' wailed Tiptoe. 'The baby was so frightened. And now I've nowhere to go tonight.'

'Get into my basket,' said Jimbo. 'It's nice and

warm. I'll go and find that rat myself.'

'But, Jimbo – have you ever caught a rat?' asked Tiptoe, settling down in the basket with the baby and cuddling up against Jimbo's warm fur. 'Rats are fierce. They bite sharply. They hang on to you and won't let go.'

'I've never caught a rat,' said Jimbo. 'I've caught mice though. And I'll go after that rat even if he flies at me and bites me. I won't have rats behaving like that to pixies like you! Now, you stay here in the warm and I'll go after that rat!'

He left Tiptoe and padded away to the woods. It was dark, but Jimbo didn't mind. He could see very well indeed in the dark. He came to the bank where the pixie had her home. A small voice called to him.

'Are you Jimbo? I'm Tiptap, Tiptoe's husband. That rat is still in our home – and, oh, dear, look at all our lovely furniture scattered everywhere!'

'How can I get the rat out of his hole?' asked Jimbo.

'Well, a squeaking mouse would bring him out,'

said Tiptap. 'But no mouse will go near that hole tonight! The rat feasts on mice. So shall I tell you what I'll do?'

'What?' asked Jimbo.

'I'll squeak like a mouse – like a baby mouse,' said Tiptap. 'That will wake up the rat and bring him out in a rush. Then you must pounce. But be careful – rats are strong and fierce and afraid of nothing.'

'Squeak away!' said Jimbo, hiding behind a big stone.

And Tiptap squeaked, '*Eeeee! Eeeee! Eeeee!*' It was a little high squeak that sounded exactly like a baby mouse's.

The rat awoke. He stirred in his hole. Tiptap squeaked again, a little nearer the hole.

The rat pricked up his ears. He sidled to the entrance of the hole. He saw a movement outside, and he pounced! The pixie fled under a stone, still squeaking. The rat had now come right out of the hole.

And then Jimbo pounced! But the rat heard him and fled, his long tail flying straight out behind him.

Jimbo raced after him, crashing through the bracken and the heather. This way and that the rat turned, and then ran down a hole too small for Jimbo to follow after.

Jimbo put his face right up to the hole.

'If you dare to go near Tiptoe's hole again I'll catch you!' he cried. 'I'm here! I'll always be around, watching for you! One day you will be my dinner. So make sure you keep away!'

The rat shook and shivered and made no sound at all! He could smell cat, he could almost feel claws on him. Never again would he turn a pixie out of a hole.

Jimbo went back to the hole and called Tiptap.

'I didn't catch him, but he's gone,' he said. 'I don't think he'll come again.'

'We'll have to spray it with bluebell perfume to get the rat smell out of it,' said Tiptap. 'You are very kind, Jimbo. Let me ride on your back, please. I'm very tired.'

So Tiptap climbed up on Jimbo's back and rode all

the way to the veranda, bumping up and down as he went. He rather enjoyed it. Tiptoe and Tippy the baby were fast asleep in Jimbo's basket. Tiptap crept in beside him. Then Jimbo put in first one paw, then another, and then the rest of his body. He lowered himself down carefully.

Soon he was asleep too, the three pixies cuddled into his fur. When Jimbo awoke, they were gone! They had all gone home to the hole in the bank to see if they could put their furniture back and hang up their curtains again. The rat had spoilt the carpet of moss, so they had to get another.

When Jimbo went to see them later that day they were settled comfortably in their little home again, and they gave him a wonderful welcome.

'What a pity you're too big to come and stay with us,' said Tiptoe. 'The baby does like you so much.'

'Well, perhaps if you and Tiptap go away for a holiday, you'd let me have the baby to take care of,' said Jimbo. 'He could sleep in my basket, and I'd give him rides on my back. We could have such fun at night when I go hunting.'

And, now I come to think of it, it must be Tippy's little feet I sometimes hear pattering at night, down on the veranda below my bedroom! Because, as you know, Jimbo is my cat.

The Fairy in the Pram

The Fairy in the Pram

'MOLLIE, I want you to take this bundle of clean lace to Mrs Button,' said Mother. 'I've washed it nicely for her and she has promised me half a crown for doing it. The money will pay for us to go to the town tomorrow, and see your Aunt Minna.'

'Oh, Mother, how lovely!' said Mollie, and she danced round in excitement. She loved going to Auntie Minna's, for there were always chocolate buns for tea, two kinds of jam, and perhaps pink jelly in a little glass cup. Then there were Auntie Minna's six goldfish in a large tank, Ginger the big cat who could open the door himself, and Poll the parrot who could say all sorts of things.

'I do like going to Auntie Minna's,' said Mollie. 'I'll take the lace to Mrs Button's for you, Mother, and bring back the half crown.'

'Be careful not to lose it,' said her mother. She gave Mollie a big parcel of lace, and the little girl ran to her doll's pram with it.

'I'll take my doll for a walk too,' she said. 'Angelina can sit at one end of the pram, and the bundle of lace can go at the other end. I'll go through the wood, Mother, so I shan't be very long, because that's a short way to Mrs Button's.'

Off she went, wheeling her doll's pram, her doll Angelina sitting up very straight with her feet resting on the bundle of lace. Mollie took the path through the wood, and in twenty minutes' time came to Mrs Button's farm.

Mrs Button was pleased to have her lace back, and gave Mollie the half crown to give to her mother. The little girl slipped it into her pocket and then turned her pram round to go home. She pushed it through the wood, thinking happily of the next day when she would see Auntie Minna, the goldfish, the cat and the parrot.

Halfway through the wood she stopped and felt in her pocket to see if the money was safe – and, oh, dear me, what do you think? There was a hole there, and the half crown had slipped out! There was no money there at all. Mollie had lost the half crown!

'Oh!' she cried in a fright. 'It's gone! Whatever will Mother say? We shan't be able to go to Auntie Minna's after all!'

She began to look for the money, but although she went almost all the way back to Mrs Button's, she couldn't find it. The grass was thick, and it was very difficult to find anything so small as a silver piece. Mollie was dreadfully upset. She wheeled her pram homewards again, crying bitterly.

Suddenly she stopped. What was that noise she heard? Surely there was someone else crying nearby too? The little girl listened. Yes, someone was sobbing not very far away. She left her pram on the path and ran to see who it was.

And what a surprise she got! Sitting on the grass holding her ankle was a fairy! She was dressed in red creeper leaves, and had orange wings, one of which was drooping down as if it were hurt.

'Ooh!' said Mollie, stopping short. 'It's a fairy! I've never seen one before.'

She hardly liked to go any nearer, but soon the fairy saw her and called her.

'Oh, little girl!' she cried. 'Do come and help me.'

Mollie ran up to her.

'What's the matter?' she asked.

'I've hurt my wing and sprained my ankle,' said the fairy, showing Mollie a swollen foot. 'I can't fly, and I can't walk, and I'm frightened of being left here all by myself in case a witch comes by.'

'How can I help you?' asked Mollie. 'Would you like me to bathe your ankle?'

'All I want is to get home to my sister,' said the fairy, drying her eyes. 'She will soon make me better. Could you take me?'

'But you can't walk,' said Mollie, 'and you're just a bit too big for me to carry.'

The fairy began to cry again. Suddenly Mollie had a bright idea.

'I know!' she cried. 'I'll wheel you to your home in my doll's pram! I've got it just nearby. Wait a minute!'

Off she ran, and soon brought her pram to where the fairy sat. She put Angelina at the other end, and then gently lifted the hurt fairy into the seat.

'This is lovely!' said the little creature. 'Oh, you *are* a nice little girl. I hope I shan't be too heavy.'

'Not a bit!' said Mollie. 'Now, which way do I go?'

'Take that tiny path over there,' said the fairy, pointing. So Mollie wheeled her pram down the little path, and at last she came to the tiniest house she had ever seen, built of white pebbles.

The door flew open as she came near, and another fairy looked out. She ran to the pram and kissed her sister.

'Have you hurt yourself?' she asked. 'Oh, what a kind little girl to bring you home safely! Come into our house, little girl, and let me give you some lemonade and honey cakes.'

So Mollie went into the little house and ate some delicious honey cakes and drank a tiny glassful of lemonade, while the hurt fairy's foot and wing were bound up in silvery bandages.

'There! That's done!' said the fairy's sister at last, and she smiled at Mollie. 'Why, little girl!' she said. 'You look as if *you've* been crying too. What was the matter?'

Then Mollie told her all about the lost half crown, and the tears came into her eyes again as she thought of what her mother would say.

'Never mind!' said the fairy. 'I can help you.'

'How?' asked Mollie.

'Well, you know, my sister and I are in charge of all the rabbits in this wood,' said the fairy. 'They have to do what we tell them, and we punish them if they are naughty. I'll soon find your half crown for you!'

She went to the door of the little pebble house and blew on a tiny reed pipe. Almost at once scores and scores of bunnies came running up and sat in rows and rows round the fairy. Mollie could hardly believe her eyes, they were so tame.

'Listen!' cried the fairy to the rabbits. 'A half crown has been lost in the wood. Go and find it! The one who brings it to me shall have a GREAT treat!'

At once all the rabbits disappeared, and Mollie and the fairies waited. In four minutes a little sandy bunny rushed up, most excited. In his paw he held a half crown, and Mollie jumped with joy to see it.

'Is this it?' asked the rabbit.

'Yes,' said the fairy. 'You are a good little rabbit. Now, for a GREAT treat you shall show this little girl back to the right path.'

Mollie took the half crown and put it safely in her other pocket, where there was no hole.

'Would the rabbit like a ride in my pram?' she asked.

The bunny's eyes gleamed with delight, and he hopped in in a trice. He covered himself up with the pram cover, and then Mollie said goodbye to the fairies, and thanked them very much for their kindness.

'Thank you for being so kind to *me*,' said the hurt fairy gratefully. Off went Mollie with Angelina and the little rabbit in her pram, the bunny pointing out the way with his paw. How pleased he was with his treat! Hundreds of other rabbits stared at him in surprise and envy as he went along the path wheeled in Mollie's pram.

At last they came to the part of the wood that Mollie knew, and the bunny hopped out.

'If ever you want another ride, come and knock at my back door, and I'll give you one,' said Mollie, when she said goodbye to him.

'I'll come the next full moon night!' cried the

rabbit gladly, and scuttled off.

When Mollie told her mother all that had happened, she didn't believe her.

'Well, Mother, here's the half crown,' said Mollie, giving it to her mother. 'We shouldn't be able to go to Auntie Minna's tomorrow if it hadn't been for the fairies and that clever little rabbit – and he says he's coming next full moon night for another ride in my pram, so you'll see him then!'

And now Mollie and her mother are anxiously waiting for full moon night to come. Wouldn't you like to see that little rabbit knocking at the back door? I would!

The Grumpy Goblins

The Grumpy Goblins

ALAN WAS cross and tired. He had worked hard at school all day, and then when he had got home to tea, his mother had sent him out on errands until bedtime.

'I haven't done my homework!' said Alan to his mother, when she said it was time for bed.

'Well, what homework is it?' she asked.

'I've got to think of twelve words beginning with *gr*,' said Alan. 'Miss Brown says the *gr* family is quite easy, and we must all come to school tomorrow ready to make sentences with words beginning with those two letters. So, Mummy, I must sit down and think some out.'

'Oh, you can do that in bed!' said his mother, and Alan had to go upstairs at once. He was cross because he felt sure it would be difficult to think out homework in bed – and he was right, for no sooner was he under the bedclothes, trying to think, than his mind wandered away and wouldn't even try to get hold of any *gr* words.

If only somebody would tell me a few! thought the little boy. He opened his eyes – and how he stared! What do you think he saw? He saw six funny little goblins round his bed, and one of them was holding a dog on a lead. The dog was just like Alan's own toy dog, but he seemed to be very much alive.

'Who are you?' asked Alan, sitting up.

'We're the Grumpy Goblins,' said one.

'Oh,' said Alan, 'I suppose you are always cross then.'

'We grumble,' said one.

'And we groan,' said another.

'And we grouse,' said the third.

'And we growl,' said the dog unexpectedly, and

gave a fierce growl that made Alan jump. Then the dog jumped up on to the bed, but the goblin pulled him back.

'Grab him!' said the others.

'He wants one of my biscuits!' said Alan, seeing the little dog sniffing in the direction of his box of treats.

'Greedy dog!' said the goblin who had the dog's lead.

The dog jumped back on to the foot of the bed with a grunt.

'He grunts like a pig,' said the first goblin.

'Gracious!' said the dog's master. 'Now he's grinning!' Sure enough the dog was smiling from ear to ear. Alan thought it was all most interesting.

'Do tell me why you've come to visit me,' said Alan.

'Your grievance called us,' said the goblins. 'Though gruff and grumpy and grave, we granted your wish.'

'What wish?' Alan asked sleepily.

'Well! Where's your gratitude?' snapped the

goblin. 'Come, Grumpies – and gradually – gradually – gracefully – gracefully ...'

'Gradually gracefully what?' said Alan, half asleep – but the Grumpy Goblins were gone! The dog jumped on to the bed and snuggled beside Alan. The little boy slept.

When he awoke in the morning he looked at the dog and remembered the strange goblins. 'You are my own toy dog, after all!' he said. 'I wonder what you were doing with those goblins. Oh, I think I know – you fetched them to do my homework for me. Yes, they did it all! I can write down heaps of words beginning with *gr* this morning – and I bet I'll get top marks!'

He did. Could you?

The Toy Clown and the Radio

The Toy Clown and
the Radio

THERE WAS a new radio in the playroom. It had only just arrived, and the two children were excited about it.

'You just turn that knob there, and the music plays,' said Betty.

'You can turn it if you like,' said Mummy. So Betty turned it, very slowly, and to the great astonishment of the toys, a band began to play out of the radio. The clown looked at it in great surprise. The teddy bear almost fell off the shelf, and the yellow cat was really frightened.

'Isn't it lovely?' said John. 'May Betty and I have it

on whenever we like, Mummy?'

'Yes – but not too loudly,' said Mummy. 'You must remember there are plenty of other people around, and they don't want to have to hear your radio all the time.'

The toys thought the radio was really wonderful. They were never tired of listening to it. Sometimes people spoke out of the radio, and the toys wondered how they got there. Sometimes people played the piano in the radio, and that seemed wonderful too. How could a piano get into that small radio?

At night, when the children had gone to bed, the clown looked longingly at the radio.

'It's magic,' he said to the others. 'It must be magic. How else can it have bands and things inside it? I wish I could open it and see exactly what is inside. How do you suppose you open it, Teddy?'

'Don't *think* of such a thing!' cried the bear in horror. 'You might break it.'

'I must just peep inside and see,' said the clown,

and he began to try and undo a screw at the back. The bear had to get the big sailor doll to come and help him take the clown away.

'We shall put you inside the brick box, if you don't solemnly promise you won't try to see inside the radio,' said the teddy bear. The clown didn't at all want to be put into the brick box, because there was so little room there, so he had to promise.

The next night he wanted to turn the knob that made the radio play. 'I want to see the light come on, and hear the music,' he said. '*Just* let me turn the knob!'

'What! Wake up everyone in the house and have them rushing to the room to see what's the matter?' cried the teddy bear. 'You must be mad.'

'Would they hear it?' said the clown. 'Oh, do let me try. I'll only turn the knob a tiny way then the music won't be very loud.'

'You really are very, very naughty, Clown,' said the bear. 'You are not to turn the knob at all.'

The clown was quite good for a night or two,

and then, when the toys were playing quietly in a corner, he crept over to the radio and turned the knob. The light shone inside the radio set, and a band began to play!

It was true that the music was very quiet indeed, but all the same, the toys were quite horrified! The bear and the sailor doll rushed over at once and turned off the knob. The light went out. The music stopped.

'Clown! How dare you!' cried the teddy bear. 'Are you quite, quite mad? Do you want to wake up the whole family?'

'No – and anyway the music played itself so quietly that nobody would have heard it,' said the clown. 'It is you, with your big shouting voice, that will wake up everyone! Be quiet. You are not to shout at me.'

'Shall we put him in the brick box?' said the sailor doll.

'You shan't, you shan't!' said the clown, and he ran away. He squeezed himself under the nursery piano, and nobody could get him out.

'Very well. Stay there!' said the bear. 'We shan't talk to you or play with you. You are a very bad toy.'

So nobody spoke to the clown that night, not even the little clockwork mouse, who loved to chatter to him. It was very sad. Nobody asked him to join in the games, and the clown felt very lonely indeed.

The next night it was just the same. The clown asked the bear to play catch, but the bear just looked at him and walked away. Then the clown spoke to the baby doll.

'How the moon shines tonight!' he said. But the baby doll stared at him with her big blue eyes and didn't answer a word.

The clown was offended. He walked away. 'Very well!' he called over his shoulder. 'If you won't play with me I'm going out of the room! I won't stay with such horrid toys!'

So out of the nursery door he went, while all the toys stared after him in horror. No toy ever went out of the playroom at night. Whatever was the clown thinking of to do such a thing?

The moon shone brightly, and the clown could see quite plainly where he was going. He went down the stairs, jumping them one at a time. They seemed very, very steep to him! He got down to the bottom and looked round. He had sometimes been taken downstairs by Betty. He knew there was a room called the kitchen that had a nice smell in it. Which was it?

He found the kitchen door and sidled round it. The kitchen was bright in the moonlight, and the pots and pans winked and blinked.

There may be a crumb or two on the floor, thought the clown, and he began to look under the table. Suddenly a shadow fell across the moonlit floor, and the clown looked up in surprise. Had the moon gone behind a cloud?

No, it hadn't. Somebody had put himself in front of the moon – and that somebody was getting in at the kitchen window! The clown stared in the greatest surprise. Who was this, forcing open the kitchen window in the middle of the night and getting inside?

It must be a burglar! thought the clown in dismay. *They come in the night sometimes, and steal things. Oh, whatever shall I do? My voice isn't big enough to wake everyone up. Oh, dear, oh, dear, what shall I do?*

The burglar sprang quietly to the floor and opened the larder door. He meant to have something to eat. The clown scuttled out of the kitchen as fast as his little legs would take him. The burglar saw him in the moonlight and jumped.

What's that? A rat, I suppose? he thought.

But it wasn't a rat. It was a frightened clown, hurrying upstairs as fast as he could go, climbing one step at a time. He came to the playroom and rushed round the door, panting. The toys looked at him in amazement.

'Goodness! What's the matter? Your face is quite pale!'

'It's a burglar, a burglar! Downstairs in the kitchen!' cried the clown. 'We must wake everyone up! Oh, quick, quick, make a noise, everyone.'

The teddy bear growled. The baby doll said 'Ma-ma, Ma-ma!' The pink cat squeaked, and so did the clown. The sailor doll rapped on the floor. But it was no good. No one heard them. No one woke up.

And then the clown did a most peculiar thing! He gave a little cry and rushed over to the radio set. He turned on the knob – turned it right round as far as it would go! The light went on inside the set – and, dear me, what a tremendous noise came blaring forth!

It was a man's voice, telling the midnight news – but the clown had put the radio on so loudly that it was as if the man on the wireless was shouting at the top of his voice.

'You bad clown!' cried the bear, and ran to turn it off. But the clown pushed him away.

'Don't! I'm waking up the household! I'm not naughty this time, I'm good.'

And so he was – for the shouting on the radio woke up everyone with a jump. It frightened the burglar in the kitchen, and he knocked over some saucepans with a clatter. Daddy ran downstairs with a poker and saw the burglar crouching in the larder. Quick as lightning Daddy shut the door and locked it. The burglar was a prisoner!

Then upstairs went Daddy to see what the shouting was in the playroom. He found Betty and John just turning off the radio there.

'This is what woke us up, Daddy,' said John. 'The radio. But who could have put it on?'

Nobody knew. Betty caught a gleam in the clown's eye, as he sat by the toy cupboard. Could *he* possibly have turned on the radio? Betty knew quite well she had put him back into the toy cupboard that evening – and there he was, sitting outside it! She felt sure he had been up to something!

The policemen came and collected the burglar out of the larder. Everyone went back to bed. The toys came out of the toy cupboard, dancing about in glee.

'The burglar's caught! Good old Clown!'

'You've been so good and clever that we'll forget you were naughty before!'

'*What* a noise the radio made, didn't it!'

The clown was pleased to find himself such a hero. He beamed all over his face. 'Now listen to me,' he said, 'whenever I want to turn the radio on at night *ever* so quietly you're to let me! I won't wake anyone at all. But I'M GOING TO TURN IT ON WHEN I WANT TO!'

'All right,' said the bear. 'We shan't stop you, you deserve a little reward. You really have been very, very clever.'

Everyone agreed, and the clockwork mouse felt very proud of his friend.

And now when he feels like a little music the clown turns the radio knob – very gently – and the music comes whispering out. Betty and John *will* be surprised if they hear it, won't they?

The Toad and the Spider

The Toad and the Spider

UNDER THE ivy that climbed up the low wall lived a fat toad, and nearby squatted a fat spider who caught in her web almost as many flies as the toad caught in his mouth. The toad was very clever at catching flies. His tongue was fixed to the front of his mouth instead of to the back, so he could flick it out a long way, and as it was a very sticky tongue it caught him many a bluebottle, and many a smaller fly too, that came to share the last feast of the year – the nectar in the greeny-yellow ivy blossoms.

The spider hated the toad. He caught flies that might have flown into her web. She sat under a leaf all day long and watched the toad who came out from under his stone and sat where he could best catch the flies that flew up and down the ivy.

'Why do you glare at me like that?' asked the toad, blinking his beautiful coppery eyes. 'There are more than enough flies for the two of us.'

'This is my hedge,' said the spider, glowering at the toad with all her eight eyes. 'These are *my* flies. You should go away and leave them to me.'

'Nothing of the sort,' said the toad, flicking out his tongue at a passing fly. He caught it neatly on the sticky end, blinked his eyes and swallowed. 'The flies belong to those that catch them. Mind your own business!'

'I wish I could catch *you* in my web!' said the spider ill-temperedly.

'You are welcome to try,' croaked the toad, and shot out his tongue at another fly.

The spider grumbled to herself all day long – and when night came and the toad disappeared under his stone again, an idea came into her head. She would run down to the toad's stone and weave a very thick strong web in front of it, then when the toad came out he would be caught!

She waited until she thought the toad must be asleep, and then ran down to his stone in the darkness. She quietly spun four thicknesses of web across the entrance to his hole. Then she crouched by the web and waited for the morning, rejoicing to think of the toad's dismay and discomfort when he found he was a prisoner. No more flies for him! If he tried to come out, the spider would stick her poison fangs into him and make him ill.

Morning came and the spider awaited the toad. But though she waited long he did not try to come out from his hole. 'Are you waiting for the old toad?' called a little field mouse, running by. 'He told me yesterday that he was coming out no more until next spring. He is going to sleep the cold days away comfortably in his hole. I see you have built a strong web in front for him. How pleased he will be! It will be a good protection from his enemies!'

The spider glared in anger. She hardly believed the mouse. 'I shall go in and see if he is really asleep,' she said. 'He has gone away because he was afraid.'

So she slipped into the hole and looked around. Sure enough, the toad was there, his eyes fast shut, for he was about to go into his winter sleep. But he was not *quite* asleep. He heard the eight legs of the spider running round him – and quick as thought he opened his eyes. Then out flicked his tongue – and where was the fierce spider? Quite gone!

'A nice door to my hole, and a nice meal,' croaked the toad comfortably.

The Rascally Goblin

The Rascally Goblin

ONCE UPON a time there was a little boy called Jack. He was a wonderful gardener, and you should have seen his flowers and vegetables! His sweet peas were simply marvellous, and as for his lettuces and beans, Mother said they were better than she could buy in any shop!

For his birthday his father gave him a set of garden tools. Jack was delighted!

'They are really good ones, Jack,' said his father, 'so you must take great care of them. They are not cheap little ones like those you had before. Remember that whenever you use your tools, you must clean them well before putting them away, and you must always hang them up properly in the shed, and not leave them out in the garden.'

'Oh, yes, Daddy, I'll easily remember that,' said Jack. 'I do like good tools, and I'll keep them just as bright and shining as you keep yours!'

He did. He cleaned them well each night, and hung them up neatly on pegs in the shed.

And then strange things began to happen. Jack simply couldn't understand it. One morning he went to get his spade and it wasn't hanging up by the handle on its nail – it was lying down, and was as dirty as could be!

'Well, I am quite sure I cleaned it last night!' said Jack, puzzled. 'But I must have forgotten to do it, I suppose!'

The next day when he went to get his watering can it wasn't in the shed at all! Jack hunted for it, and at last found it out in the garden. How funny! He was sure he had put it into the shed when he had last used it.

Then there came a Saturday morning, and Father was at home to do some gardening too – and do you know, when he went with Jack to the shed to get his tools, he saw all Jack's new tools lying about anyhow in the shed, each of them dirty! He looked at them in surprise.

He was very cross with Jack. 'Didn't you promise me that you would look after these beautiful new tools?' he said to Jack. 'I am disappointed in you, Jack.'

'But, Daddy, I did clean them and put them away,' said Jack.

His father frowned. 'Now, don't tell stories,' he said. 'It's bad enough to break a promise without telling untruths as well!'

Jack did not say any more. But he was very upset. He worked with his father all the morning, and when they stopped he was careful to clean his tools and hang them up nicely.

'That's right, Jack,' said Father. 'Now, listen – if I find those nice new tools lying about dirty again,

I shall take them away, and you will have to use your old ones instead!'

Poor Jack! He knew that he always did put his tools away properly. He couldn't think how it was that they became dirty.

But the tools knew! When they were safely in the shed at night they talked to one another.

'It's a shame that Jack is blamed for what that rascally goblin does!' said the watering can.

'Yes,' said the spade, swinging to and fro on its nail. 'He comes along and borrows us at night for his gardening, and never thinks of cleaning us or hanging us up properly.'

'He's a horrid, nasty fellow,' said the little fork. 'He bent me the other day.'

'And he loaded me so full that I thought my wheel would break!' said the barrow.

'I say! Won't it be horrid if Jack's father does take us away from him, and makes him use his old tools instead,' said the trowel. 'We shall be stuck away somewhere then, and never see the sunshine! Besides, I do like being used by Jack. He does make his garden so fine with us!'

'I've got an idea!' said the wheelbarrow thoughtfully. 'Listen! I guess that rascally goblin will come along tonight. Well – let's be ready for him, shall we?'

'Ready for him? What do you mean?' asked the spade.

'Well, let's go for him and give him such a fright that he won't ever come here again!' said the barrow.

'Oooh, yes!' said the trowel. 'That would be fine. I don't mind banging him on the head!'

'And I'd love to soak him with water!' said the watering can, tilting itself up in glee.

'And I could run at him and run my wheel over his toes!' said the barrow, giving a great gurgle of laughter.

So it was all arranged. The tools got a come-alive spell from the little fairy they knew and they came alive for one night! The watering can popped outside on spindly legs and filled itself at the tap! The spade hopped to the garden beds and filled itself full of earth. The barrow filled itself full of potatoes from a sack in the shed. The fork and the trowel practised jumping down from their nails, so that they might be ready when the great moment came!

Even the hosepipe joined in and said it would pretend to be a big snake! Oh, dear! What fun they were going to have!

'Shh! Shh! Here comes the rascally goblin!' said the barrow suddenly. The shed door opened and a little head, with big pointed ears, looked in. Then the goblin ran inside and looked round for the tools.

'Where are you, spade? Where are you, barrow?' he said. 'I've got a lot of digging to do tonight and a lot of watering too!'

'Here I am!' said the spade, and jumping up from the floor, where it had been lying ready with its spadeful of earth, it shot the earth all over the surprised goblin!

'Oooh! What's that?' said the goblin, alarmed.

The trowel jumped off its nail and hit him on the head, and the fork jumped too, and pricked him on the leg. The goblin scrambled up and ran for the door.

But the hosepipe was there, wriggling about like a big green snake!

'Oooh! Ow! Snakes!' yelled the frightened goblin. 'Get away, snakes!'

But the hosepipe was thoroughly enjoying itself. It wriggled along after the goblin and wound itself round his leg. The barrow laughed so much that it could hardly stand! Then it suddenly ran at the goblin, wheeled itself over his toe, and emptied all the potatoes over him. Plop, thud, bang, crash! How astonished that goblin was! He sat among the potatoes and yelled for help – but there was no one to hear him.

Then along came the watering can, and lifted itself up into the air. Pitter-patter, pitter-patter! The water poured all over the goblin as the can watered him well!

He ran to a corner, but the can followed him and soaked him wherever he went.

The hosepipe laughed so much that it forgot to be a snake by the door and the goblin tore out of the shed and made for home. He was wet and dirty and bruised and bumped.

'There were witches and snakes in that shed tonight,' wept the goblin, when he was safe at home. 'I'll never go there again, never, never, never!'

He never did, so Jack was not scolded any more for dirty tools. They were always clean and bright, hanging neatly in their places. But oh, how they laugh each night when they remember how they punished that rascally goblin! I do wish I'd been there to see it all, don't you?

A Good Little
Messenger

A Good Little
Messenger

'WE SIMPLY must get this necklace to the Princess Peronel before the party tonight,' said Bron the elf.

'Yes. What a nuisance that we've lost the way!' said Jinks. 'It's night-time now, and all the birds except the owls have gone to roost. We can't ask even a swallow to fly with the necklace to the palace.'

'Well, I'm not going to ask the owl,' said Bron. 'He's rather fierce. If we call him, he might think we are mice down here in the dark and come swooping on us with his great talons!'

'Shall we ask a night moth?' said Jinks.

'No. They would never fly straight to the princess,'

said Bron. 'You know how they dodge about – and they so often go and fly for hours round a bright light, wasting time. No moth would get to the princess in time for the party.'

'Look – what's that flying above us?' said Jinks suddenly.

Bron looked up. 'It's a bat! Perhaps *he* would take it. Has he any paws to hold the necklace in?'

'I don't know,' said Jinks. 'Let's call him down and ask him.'

So they called to the little bat who was flying among the trees, dodging and turning deftly in the air. He flew down at once with a little high squeak.

'Did you call me?' he said. 'What do you want?'

'We've lost our way,' said Bron, 'and we have to take this necklace to the Princess Peronel for her to wear at a dance tonight. We wondered if you knew the way and could take it.'

'Of course I know the way,' said the bat.

'How can you take it then?' asked Jinks. 'Have

you little paws – or fingers like ours?'

'No. I've no fingers at all,' said the bat. 'I've changed them into wings – look!'

And he suddenly opened his black wings in front of Jinks and Bron. They stared at them in surprise.

'Why, what have you done with your fingers?' said Jinks, amazed.

'I've grown my finger bones very, very long indeed,' said the bat proudly. 'And I've grown a kind of black webbing between them, to make myself wings! Isn't it clever?'

'Yes, very clever,' said Jinks, astonished. The elves looked at the curious, webbed wings – yes, they were just long finger bones with black skin between. How strange!

'No feathers, you see,' said the bat. 'But, of course, as I've made wings out of my fingers, I've no front paws – no hands like you have! You can't have both!'

'What's that hook-like thing at the tip of your wings?' asked Jinks curiously.

'Oh, that? It's all that's left of my thumb,' said the bat. 'It's quite useful. I use it to hang myself up with when I'm tired.'

'You're a clever creature, and an odd one,' said Bron. 'But I don't think you'll be any help to us, Bat – because you can't hold this precious necklace with your wings – or your hook-like thumbs! And your hind legs are no use for that either.'

'We've called you down to us for nothing,' said Jinks. 'We never dreamt that you bats had changed your fingers into wings!'

'I *could* help you,' said the bat. 'I *could* take that necklace for you. I know I could.'

'You couldn't,' said Bron. 'You might drop it, and that would never do. Now, if only you had a *pocket* – a nice sensible *pocket* . . .'

The bat gave a high little squeak. 'I *have* got a pocket!' he said. 'I really have!'

'You haven't!' said Jinks, looking closely at him. 'Bats don't have pockets. Kangaroos do, so I've heard, and bees have pockets in their knees, and ...'

'And *I've* got one, I really have!' said the bat. 'Look, it's here – a little pouch between my legs and my tail. A very good pocket indeed!'

The elves looked at it. 'So it is!' said Jinks. 'Bron, do you think it's big enough to hold the necklace safely?'

'Try it and see,' said the bat, and Bron took the shining necklace and stuffed it gently into his little pocket.

'There, it's just right!' said the bat. 'Well, I'll go now – and I'll fly straight to the palace, I promise you! Goodbye!'

He was off and into the air before the elves could say a word. They watched him flying off in the moonlight, a black-winged shadow.

'Well! I've learnt something tonight!' said Jinks. 'I never knew how bat wings were made before – out of finger bones. Would you believe it!'

'And very good wings they are too,' said Bron. He

looked at his own hands. 'I wonder if *we* could grow wings by using our fingers?' he said. 'No. We can't. Do you think we were wise to trust that little bat with the necklace, Jinks?'

'Oh, yes,' said Jinks. 'Perhaps he'll be back sometime tonight to tell us he delivered it safely.'

He was right. Two hours later the bat was back again, flying swiftly on his finger-wings. He flew down to the elves.

'I gave it to the princess!' he said. 'She is wearing it now. She looks *beautiful*! It was safe in my pocket all the way!'

Acknowledgements

All efforts have been made to seek necessary permissions.

The stories in this publication first appeared in the following publications:

'Giant Sleepyhead and the Magic Towers' first appeared in *Merry Moments Annual 1926*, published by George Newnes in 1925.

'The Cold, Cold Nose' first appeared in *The Teachers World*, No. 1594, 1933.

'The Tricks of Rag and Tag' first appeared in *Sunny Stories for Little Folks*, No. 51, 1928.

'The Very Old Teddy Bear' first appeared in *The Enid Blyton Pennant Readers 9*, published by Macmillan in 1950.

'Chipperdee's Scent' first appeared in *Sunny Stories for Little Folks*, No. 186, 1934.

'What's Happened to the Clock?' first appeared in *Enid Blyton's Sunny Stories*, No. 445, 1948.

'The Tale of Lanky-Panky' first appeared in *Enid Blyton's Sunny Stories*, No. 96, 1938.

'The Donkey Who Bumped His Head' first appeared in *Sunny Stories for Little Folks*, No. 78, 1929.

'The Cuckoo in the Clock' first appeared in *Sunny Stories for Little Folks*, No. 101, 1930.

'The Lucky Green Pea' first appeared in *Sunny Stories for Little Folks*, No. 93, 1930.

'Hotels for the Birds' first appeared in *The Enid Blyton Nature Readers No. 36*, published by Macmillan in 1955.

'The Magic Needle' first appeared in *Enid Blyton's Sunny Stories*, No. 531, 1952.

'The Forgotten Rabbit' first appeared in *Sunny Stories for Little Folks*, No. 202, 1934.

'Pippitty's Pink Paint' first appeared in *Merry Moments Annual 1926*, published by George Newnes in 1925.

'Mr Twiddle and the Cat' first appeared in *Enid Blyton's Sunny Stories*, No. 177, 1940.

'Snifty's Lamppost' first appeared as 'Snifty's Lamp Post' in *Sunny Stories for Little Folks*, No. 47, 1928.

'The Foolish Green Frog' first appeared in *Sunny Stories for Little Folks*, No. 192, 1934.

'The Little Paper Boats' first appeared in *Sunny Stories for Little Folks*, No. 191, 1934.

'The Little Clockwork Mouse' first appeared in *Enid Blyton's Sunny Stories*, No. 39, 1937.

'Mr Dozey's Dream' first appeared in *The Evening Standard*, No. 38,891, published by The Evening Standard Company Ltd. in 1949.

'You Help Me, and I'll Help You' first appeared as 'You Help Me and I'll Help You!' in *Enid Blyton's Sunny Stories*, No. 516, 1951.

'The Fairy in the Pram' first appeared in *Sunny Stories for Little Folks*, No. 124, 1931.

'The Grumpy Goblins' first appeared in *The Teachers World*, No. 1843, 1938.

'The Toy Clown and the Radio' first appeared as 'The Golliwog and the Wireless' in *Sunny Stories for Little Folks*, No. 300, 1943.

'The Toad and the Spider' first appeared in *The Teachers World*, No. 1743, 1936.

'The Rascally Goblin' first appeared in *Enid Blyton's Sunny Stories*, No. 34, 1937.

'A Good Little Messenger' first appeared in *The Enid Blyton Nature Readers No. 36*, published by Macmillan in 1955.

Also available:

Enid Blyton

STORIES OF
MAGIC
AND
MISCHIEF

30
stories

A spellbinding selection of magical and
mischievous tales by the world's
best-loved storyteller!

Enid Blyton

NATURE STORIES

30 stories

Explore the great outdoors with these short stories by the world's best-loved storyteller!

ENIDBLYTON.CO.UK
IS FOR PARENTS, CHILDREN AND TEACHERS!

Sign up to the newsletter on the homepage for a monthly round-up of news from the world of

JOIN US ON SOCIAL MEDIA

f **EnidBlytonOfficial**   **🐦** **BlytonOfficial**

Enid Blyton

is one of the most popular children's authors of all time. Her books have sold over 500 million copies and have been translated into other languages more often than any other children's author.

Enid Blyton adored writing for children. She wrote over 700 books and about 2,000 short stories. *The Famous Five* books, now 80 years old, are her most popular. She is also the author of other favourites including *The Secret Seven*, *The Magic Faraway Tree*, *Malory Towers* and *Noddy*.

Born in London in 1897, Enid lived much of her life in Buckinghamshire and loved dogs, gardening and the countryside. She was very knowledgeable about trees, flowers, birds and animals.

Dorset – where some of the Famous Five's adventures are set – was a favourite place of hers too.

Enid Blyton's stories are read and loved by millions of children (and grown-ups) all over the world. Visit enidblyton.co.uk to discover more.

Illustration by
Laura Ellen Anderson.